ROGUE ROYALTY

MEGHAN

MARCH

Visit my website at www.meghanmarch.com

CONTENTS

ABOUT *ROGUE ROYALTY*

Unthinkable. Unbelievable. Inconceivable.

I don't recognize what my life has become. I can't tell where the lies end and the truth begins anymore.

He came into my world and urged me out of my safe little corner.

All my dreams are coming true except the one thing I want most—my own happy ending.

But I'll fight for it.

For now.

For always.

Rogue Royalty is the final book in the Savage Trilogy.

ONE

TEMPERANCE

I sit on the chair, birds chirping in the trees above me, and I feel nothing.

Nothing.

I'm supposed to feel something. There are five stages to grief. I read about them in the paperwork the funeral home gave me.

Denial, anger, bargaining, depression, and acceptance.

Where the hell is *feeling nothing* on that list?

Why can't I be angry? Rage would be so much easier than this . . . emptiness.

I'm broken.

Steam has long since stopped rising from the tea in the china cup Harriet pressed into my hands, but I haven't yet taken my first sip.

My landlady returns from the house, a tie-dyed silk

caftan billowing out around her in the breeze, and an envelope in her hand.

"Temperance, darling. There was a man here for you."

Every muscle in my body tenses. "What man?" I whisper.

"I already forget his name. Something that ended in Stein and sounded exceptionally snobby."

Cell by cell, I force myself to relax. *Breathe, Temperance. In. Out. In. Out.*

It's been my mantra during the hellacious month since my brother's funeral, and there's been more than one day when iron fists clutched my lungs and tried to suffocate me.

I wanted them to suffocate me. Sometimes I still do.

I never knew breathing could hurt so much. But when you've been flayed open and gutted, even existing hurts.

"I think he got tired of buzzing your apartment. He said he's been trying to reach you for days."

I ignore the buzzing when I'm upstairs. I think people have come, based on the food showing up in my fridge when I remember to think about eating, but everything is such a blur that I couldn't tell you who it was or how long ago they came. It's better that way. I don't want to see anyone. I didn't even want to come outside to have tea with Harriet, but she threatened to evict me if I didn't see the sunlight at least once this month.

Harriet sets a manila envelope on the table. "He didn't want to leave this with me, but I told him he could deliver it through me or shove it up his sphincter, because you wouldn't be answering your bell even if the four horsemen of the apocalypse rang. He relented after I promised you wouldn't sue for allowing me to forge your signature."

I force a rusty noise from my throat that's supposed to be a laugh, because that seems like the normal human reaction to Harriet's statement. *Normal.* Something else I'll never be again.

I look down at the envelope where my name is typed in bold capital letters above my address. Because I'm not yet ready to meet Harriet's undoubtedly concerned gaze, I glance at the upper left corner.

The sender is three last names I don't recognize, but they all sound fancy.

"I've never heard of these people."

"He said he works for a lawyer's office." Her finger jabs into my field of vision as she points at the envelope. "For this lawyer's office."

Lawyers.

Great.

I turn away from the envelope and resume staring at the Chinese lantern hanging from a tree branch, and let the muted street noise wash over me.

I decide I like the sound out here. Silence is the enemy. Silence means I can hear my own thoughts, and I can't face those yet.

I can't face any of it yet.

"Aren't you going to open it?" Harriet's tone vibrates with impatience.

"No."

"Dammit, girl. You can't ignore the entire world forever."

I nod like I'm agreeing with her, but in reality, I plan to ignore the world for as long as humanly possible. Forever, if I can.

It's kept spinning, even though my universe has crashed to a halt. It will keep spinning while I drown myself in grief.

"If you won't, then I will." She snatches the envelope off the wrought-iron table and rips it open. "Not like it's my first federal offense of the week," she says as she pulls papers out of it.

Harriet mumbles to herself for a few minutes, and I purposely block out what she's saying. I don't care what it says. I don't care about anything. It's easier that way.

Then she says something I can't ignore.

". . . the building and all of its contents are now solely owned by Temperance Ransom."

I tear my gaze off the lantern and stare at the paper in Harriet's hand. "What?"

She holds it out to me, and I gape at it. At first, the words on the page blur together, and I swipe at my eyes to clear my vision. My fingers come away wet.

I'm not crying.

I've perfected the art of lying to myself. I suppose

that seems fitting, considering I've been drowning in lies for months, even though I didn't know it.

I blink and focus on the words on the page.

A voice inside me screams *No!* but I shut it down. This letter confirms one more fact. The one I refused to believe was true. Because I'm stupid.

Kane is never coming back.

Whatever was left inside me, holding together my last shreds of hope that I was wrong about everything, snaps. I crumple the paper as I rock in the chair with tears pouring down my face.

TWO
TEMPERANCE

For hours, I stare at the letter—smoothed-out but still battered—where it lies on the coffee table. My vision goes blurry until I blink every so often.

Kane left me the warehouse.

How dare he?

For the first time since I opened my eyes to face the reality that my brother, Rafe, was gone, I feel something other than a vast and yawning *nothing*.

Anger.

It's there. Simmering in my soul, warming up to a roaring boil.

How dare he?

I bolt off the sofa and pace the tiny living room and kitchen space of my apartment. Pacing isn't normally my thing—it's Keira's. But right now, I feel pent-up anger hit my bloodstream like an addict mainlining her latest score. I can't hold still.

Kane gave me the motherfucking building and all the cars. Like that somehow, some way, on any planet, makes up for the fact that he *killed my goddamned brother.*

An animalistic howl rips free from my lungs as tears once again spill forth.

"How could you do this? *I hate you!*"

Grief takes me to my knees and I pound on the floor, not caring what Harriet must think below me.

I beat the scarred wood until my fists feel bruised to the bone. Dropping my forehead to the floor, I sob.

"How could you do this?" The words come out as barely a whisper, because I have nothing left.

He took everything from me.

A pile of bricks filled with hunks of metal means nothing now.

Nothing.

Someone knocks on my door. "Temperance, it's Harriet—"

"I'm okay," I reply, my voice cracking.

"You have a visitor."

"No!" I bark out my answer. I don't want to see anyone. Can't see anyone.

"It's your boss, dear."

Great. Just who I want to see me like this.

I collapse into a pathetic heap on the floor. The door opens before I can find the energy to rise to my feet.

"Temperance? Oh, honey. I'm so sorry."

Keira's heels click over to me, and she drops to her

7

knees beside me before wrapping an arm around my shoulders.

I haven't seen her since my brother's funeral—although I think she's been here while I was sleeping twenty hours a day. She told me to take as much time as I need and that everything would be fine at the distillery.

I took her at her word, forgetting completely about the responsibilities I used to be proud of handling, and wallow in hell instead.

"What can I do?" she whispers, and I hate the pity in her voice. But why wouldn't she pity me? I'm the dumbass who fell for the guy who killed her own brother.

I'm a joke. A disaster. A mess beyond all hot messes.

I swallow and try to think of something to say. Anything.

"He gave me a building." I sit up and stare straight ahead, not meeting her gaze.

"What?" she asks.

"He gave me a motherfucking building!" I reach for the shreds of paper on the floor in front of me. "How could he do this to me? He lied, and I believed him. How could I have been so fucking stupid? How?"

My reserve of tears should be empty, but they flow faster and faster. I ball my sore hands into fists again and try to wipe the droplets away.

Keira hugs me, squeezing tight. "I'm so sorry. I'm so sorry." She repeats the words over and over, rocking with me as I bawl like someone who had her heart ripped out. And I did.

To top it off, it was my own damned fault.

I might as well have pulled the trigger myself. Rafe died because of me. He came because of me. Kane lied to me. Used me. *Betrayed me.*

The wounds are still too fresh.

"How could he do that?"

"I don't know, honey. I truly don't."

I whip my head sideways, almost cracking skulls with Keira. "But Mount knew. Didn't he?"

"Temp—"

I cut off whatever she's about to say. "Don't you come here and give me some bullshit story. *He had to know. He knows everything.*"

Keira swallows, pity creasing her features. "He hasn't told me anything. I swear it to you on my life. Lachlan could've known, but he would never tell me. I don't even know who gave you a building."

I stare at her in shock. *She doesn't know who Kane is?* How is that even possible?

Mount. Mount is the reason for all of this.

Every bit of pain I'm feeling right now can be laid at his doorstep for sending Kane into my life. But I can't hate Keira for that. She didn't do anything wrong— except marry the devil.

"Mount had to know everything."

Keira closes her eyes for a beat. "You're probably right. He probably knew. There's very little he doesn't know. However, there's a lot he doesn't share, and always for good reason."

"I hate him!" The words come out a raw roar. "I fucking hate them all."

"I know. I'm sorry, Temperance. So sorry."

Shredded inside, I drop my gaze back to the paper on the floor. "I want answers."

"I know you do, and I can't give you what I don't have."

"He told me he wouldn't do it," I whisper, even though she has no idea who I'm talking about. "How could he do it?"

"I don't know."

I reach for the paper and crush it in my hands. "I feel so fucking stupid. I trusted a *hit man*. Who does that?"

Keira stays silent beside me, either because now she knows who I'm talking about, or because she trusts the man who orders hit men to pull the trigger. Either way, it doesn't change anything.

"I can't get over feeling so stupid. Like I brought this on myself. If I'd just—"

"Shh." Keira interrupts. "You can't relive it over and over, thinking *what if?*"

I turn to meet her gaze. "I know. I just wish . . ." I shake my head and look down again. I can't face her pity. It's too heavy.

I clear my throat. "When do you need me to come back to work? I know I've taken more time than I should have." Even as I make the offer, I cringe at the thought of going back and facing everyone.

"Don't worry about that. Take all the time you need. I hired someone to help out, and things are going fine. You don't need to worry about anything but you."

"Are you sure?" Relief rolls through me.

"Yes. Absolutely. Seven Sinners isn't going anywhere. Is there anything you need? Anything at all I can do to help?"

I'm quiet for several beats.

"I want to talk to Mount." I lock eyes with Keira. "I need to talk to Mount."

After a few moments, she replies quietly, "Then I'll make it happen."

THREE
TEMPERANCE

N o one in their right mind begs for an audience with the bogeyman, but I've long since quit thinking of myself as sane.

My buzzer rings, and I walk to the intercom.

"Yes?"

There's a grunt in response. No words. But the grunt tells me all I need to know.

My ride is here, and my driver is a man who doesn't speak. V.

I'm going to face the devil himself and demand answers. If only I could demand that he bring my brother back. That's all I want.

That and to shed this heavy cloak of betrayal that weighs down my every step.

Kane lied to me.

I believed him.

I hate myself for that. Maybe even more than I hate him.

"I'm on my way down," I say into the intercom, like there's any chance I'm going to miss this meeting.

I shove my feet into battered work boots. They fit with my ripped jeans and old T-shirt. It's the best I can manage.

When I opened my closet earlier to find something to wear, a memory of scanning the very same clothes to find something to wear to the club hits me.

To wear to the club to meet him.

I slammed the door shut and scooped something off my floor.

At least jeans and a T-shirt don't make me want to crawl back into bed and give up on the world like a skirt or dress would. Everything makes me think of him and all the mistakes I made. How easily I was played.

And now, nothing will ever be the same.

I leave my apartment, locking the door behind me, and plod down the spiral staircase.

Harriet's windows are open, and an opera I have zero chance of naming floats out onto the evening air.

I stop and tell her I'm leaving, but I don't want to talk more than necessary. I realize I'm being awful to everyone who gives the tiniest damn about me. That list is short to begin with, so I should be kinder and more grateful, but I just don't have it in me right now.

I hate myself for that too.

With a deep breath, I make my way down the brick

walkway to the gate, where I see V, Keira's driver and bodyguard, standing beside a black car.

The car.

I almost puke my guts up on the brick pathway when I realize it's the Maybach I rode to the airport in with Kane. On the way to meet my brother to flee the country. But really, there was no trip planned. Only my brother's execution.

Mount knows I rode in this car.

Fucking asshole. Is this his way of testing me? Forcing me to relive it? Making me decide how badly I want to see him and get my answers?

I wrap my fingers around the wrought-iron bars and stare at V. He stares back at me, expressionless.

I can't do this.

He lifts his chin, crosses his arms, and waits.

I hate him too.

Swallowing the bile rising in my throat, I release the bars and reach for the latch.

I can do this. I have no choice.

Silently, I cross the sidewalk, and V turns to open the back door for me.

I freeze as soon as I see the interior. I swear I can smell Kane's uniquely spicy scent in the air.

Stop being so dramatic, Temperance. Get in the fucking car.

I berate myself for my weakness, just like I've berated myself for everything else over the last month. If I'd had a whip, my skin would be ribbons.

I get in the car and squeeze my eyes shut as he closes me inside. On the seat next to me is a black hood.

No fucking way.

When the front door closes, V grunts and my gaze snaps to the rearview mirror. He nods, and I know what he wants. He wants me to put it on.

Just like Kane made me wear the beanie.

"And if I don't?" I ask.

He points to the gate I just came out.

"I hate you," I tell him. It's juvenile and makes me a bitch, but I don't care.

Memories come tumbling back as I grab the black hood and pull it over my head.

"So, where to? The bat cave?"

My naive quip of a question from weeks ago sucker punches me in the gut as the world goes dark.

Now the fucking bat cave is mine, and all I want to do is burn it to the ground. *And maybe I will.*

The drive to Mount's compound is quick, as I expected. I know it's in the French Quarter, but I've never been there. It's not exactly a place people are invited to.

When V opens the back door, I reach for the hood, and when I don't hear a grunt, I tug it off.

He nods and jerks his chin to the side, indicating I should get out. I follow him through a door and up a windowless set of stairs and down several corridors. It reminds me of the club.

No. No, it does not. It's nothing like it.

When he pushes a hidden button and the wall in front of us moves, I jerk back.

Now, this reminds me more of a bat cave.

Again, a slice of betrayal shears through me. I follow V and find myself in some kind of library office. Heavy bookcases line the walls, and a large wooden desk dominates the space in front of me.

Mount sits behind the desk, scrawling something on a piece of paper before he folds it and shoves it in an envelope.

A soft whoosh comes from behind me, and I whip around to see Scar exit through the spinning fireplace door.

What the hell?

I've finished surveying the contents of the room— two leather chairs, a few lamps, and a sideboard with decanters of liquor—when Mount finally looks up.

"I don't take meeting requests, Ms. Ransom. I'm humoring you only for the sake of my wife. Tread carefully."

Under normal circumstances, I'd be shaking in my boots, literally. But now? I have nothing to lose. Absolutely nothing.

Suddenly, all the questions I desperately want answered fly out of my head, leaving only one.

"Why?" It sounds like someone dragged the word from my throat with rusty pliers.

His black gaze narrows on me. "Why what?"

"Why did you do it? Did you want my brother dead? Is that it?"

Mount leans back in his chair and crosses his arms over his chest. The fit of his custom-tailored suit reminds me too much of Kane, and I have to force myself not to look away.

"You have my condolences on the loss of your brother, Ms. Ransom."

"That's not why I'm—"

He cuts me off with a glare. "If I'd wanted Ransom dead, he would've been. As for why I did any of it? I don't need to explain myself, but I will say that you getting kidnapped and killed would've made my wife unhappy. Keeping you safe was the only way to avoid that."

The rage that started building in me earlier comes to a head as I stalk toward his desk.

"But you had to know about the plan to kill Rafe!"

Mount rises to his feet and plants his fists on the desk in front of him. "What I knew then or know now is none of your fucking business."

A sob chokes me, cutting off my ability to respond, and my knees give out. I stumble backward and land in a chair, rocking forward as the tears come again.

I don't care that I'm crying in Mount's office. I don't care about anything but the gaping wounds tearing me apart.

"You're going to make yourself sick crying like that."

I blink through my torrent of tears to find a box of

tissues shoved onto my lap and Mount crouching in front of me.

"If you tell anyone I keep tissues in my office, I'll make sure you're never heard from again. It would destroy my reputation."

The statement is delivered deadpan and I know it's meant as humor, but I don't have any to spare right now. I take a tissue from the box and blow my nose.

"You're not helping yourself by wallowing in your grief, Temperance. I told you before, you're cut from the same cloth as my wife. That means you will find that last reserve of strength, put some steel in your spine, and stand up. You're not dead. Quit acting like it."

My tears dry up. "Don't pretend you know me. Don't pretend you have any idea how it feels—"

"It doesn't matter what I know or how you feel. You want to crawl into that coffin with your brother? Feel free. But you will not drag my wife down with you. I'll make sure you're cut loose long before that."

I jerk back. "What do you mean?"

"Right now, you're making her sad. I eliminate things that make Keira sad. Do you understand me?"

My jaw hangs open. "Are you seriously threatening to kill me because I upset Keira? After watching my brother *die* in front of me?"

I remember my confrontation with Gregor Standish, and how I worried for him because of what he said about Keira . . . and then he died. There's no question in my mind that Mount was responsible for his death because of Standish's attack on her and the distillery.

My question goes unanswered, but I know Mount's response would be a resounding *yes*. There's nothing he wouldn't do for Keira.

I wanted that, even though I didn't know I wanted it. Another pang of grief and anger tears into me.

"Get up. Wipe off the tears. Get your life together. And don't go back to Seven Sinners until you can talk without screaming or crying. Do you understand me?"

Mount is harsh and brutal, and part of me hates him for it. The other part . . . the other part knows I needed to hear it. I reach out to grasp his wrist before he walks away.

His gaze flicks down to where I'm touching him and moves back to my face.

"No matter how much I needed to hear that, I still hate you for whatever part you played in this."

"Duly noted." He tugs his wrist free from my grip. "You're excused, Ms. Ransom."

FOUR
TEMPERANCE

Αs if through Mount's will, my tears dry up.

I'm not dead, and I have to quit acting like it.

This is the second time in a year that I've been violently reminded that life is short. *And look where me seizing the moment got me last time.*

Looking for a club where I could indulge my dirtiest fantasies, but not finding one. Then accidentally stumbling upon one and living out my fantasies with a stranger. A stranger who ended up being not just a hit man, but a hit man who had a contract to kill my brother—and promised not to fulfill that contract.

Never trust a hit man. You'd think that would be obvious, but apparently not when your name is Temperance Ransom.

I push all that aside and stare at the blank sheet in front of me.

It's time to figure out what the hell I'm going to do

next. Living in a fog of grief isn't going to work. Rafe would be so pissed at me.

Well, I'm pissed at you too, Rafe. You should have never taken that job.

I shut down that thought too.

What happened is done. Now all that's left is for me to move forward, no matter how badly I want to curl up in a ball and let myself wither away.

I'm done withering. It's time to *live.*

Squeezing the pencil between my fingers, I think of what I want most—other than my brother back. *And the other thing I refuse to put into words because I can't possibly want it.*

My mind stays completely blank.

Wow. Failing at dreaming. Excellent.

I toss the pencil down and walk to the cupboard and open it. The shelf where I keep my alcohol is empty.

Harriet.

Knowing the old woman, she only took it because she wants to draw me out of my apartment if I want to drink, not actually prevent me from drinking.

She's wily.

I stalk back to the table to snatch up the paper and pencil and head for the door.

If she's going to rob me of my booze, she may as well help me figure out where the hell I go from here.

This time, instead of opera, she's listening to Tupac when I open the back door.

"Harriet?"

She looks up from the easel in the middle of the living room where she's painting. "Steal the booze and she will come. That's what I always say."

I nod at the easel. "Am I interrupting?"

"No, I'm just inventing a new school of painting. I call it West Coast Modern."

Of course she is. Why wouldn't she? This woman has probably lived more in one year than I have in my entire life.

She notices the paper in my hand. "Grocery list?"

I shake my head. "No."

"Bucket list?"

Her second guess is eerily accurate.

"Something like that."

A smile spreads over her face. "Excellent!"

She claps her hands, and blue paint splatters on her hot pink smock before she returns the brush to a jar and comes toward me.

"What are we starting with? I mean, that is, if you want company for any of it. I've already completed three bucket lists and a fuck-it list, and I'm still not dead, so I need someone else's next." She snatches the paper from my hand and her head jerks back. "It's blank. Good Lord, Temperance. No wonder you need me so badly."

Harriet takes the pencil from my hand and lays the

paper on the counter. She scrawls something on the top line before turning it around so I can read it.

I expect it to say something insane, like *three-way with two Russian princes*, but once again, Harriet manages to shock me.

1. Be happy.

It's so simple.

I lift my gaze to hers and whisper, "Be happy."

"It's the only thing that truly matters, my dear. If you can do that, life is magical." Her faded gaze meets mine. "Darling, you're not the only one to have loved and lost. I had a family—brothers and sisters. I've outlived them all. Husbands too. Although only one at a time. Either way, loss is never easy." She covers my hand with her paint-spattered one. "But it's also never a reason to give up living yourself."

"How do you get over it?"

She squeezes my fingers. "You don't. You live with it. The pain will always be there, but in time, it won't be as sharp. One day, you'll go a minute without thinking about them. Someday, an hour. Eventually, you might live an entire day without being overwhelmed by grief. Healing takes time."

At this very moment, I can't imagine not thinking about what happened for a minute, an hour, and especially not a day. But Harriet has never lied to me, and she's clearly wiser than I am.

"So, what's next on my list?"

She releases my hand and turns toward her wine fridge. "That, my dear, only you can answer. Dream big."

It takes several glasses of champagne for me to pick up the pencil again, but by the time I leave Harriet's, I've added a few things to the list.

2. Honor my brother's memory.
3. Introduce myself as an artist.
4. Drink wine at Harriet's vineyard in Italy.
5. Travel the world.

There's one more thing I want to write down, but I'm not brave—or stupid—enough yet.

Find love again.

FIVE
TEMPERANCE

The next day, I wake up and take a shower. I've wasted a month of my life drowning in grief over things I can't change, and it's time to take a step toward my future, even if I have no idea what it holds. I put on makeup, dress in jeans and a tank top, and leave my apartment before ten o'clock.

I'm going to get coffee and a beignet, and then I need to track down the Tahoe with my sculpture. I also need to get my Bronco back, although I'm not sure I'm ready to do that. It's time to start reclaiming my life, no matter how much it hurts to think about all of those things.

On the way to the café, a prickle of unease creeps down my spine when I see a man in a baseball cap, dark glasses, and wearing all black duck into a doorway as I turn a corner and look behind me.

Am I being followed?

I rush home and slam the gate behind me with a clang before leaning against the brick and fishing out my phone. I start talking as soon as Keira answers with a cautious greeting.

"I need to talk to Mount. I need to know if they're going to come after me, because I think I'm being followed."

"Whoa. Whoa. What are you talking about?" My boss's tone takes on a panicked edge. "Where are you?"

"I'm at my apartment, but I think someone was following me when I went for coffee this morning. I thought with Rafe gone they wouldn't keep coming after me."

"I'll call him right now."

Before she hangs up, I quickly add, "Can you ask him what happened to the Tahoe and my sculpture? I'd like that back. Actually, I need it delivered to Noble Art."

Is it a lot to ask my boss? Yes. Do I care? No.

Do I have a death wish giving orders to Mount? Not exactly, but I also have nothing to lose. I won't cower and be intimidated by him or anyone else, including whoever was following me. They can fuck off too. I refuse to live in fear.

That's when I make the decision—I'm done hiding from the world. I'm going to live and live *fearlessly*.

"It's good to have you back among the living, Temperance," Keira says quietly before she hangs up.

It doesn't take long before I get a text.

26

KEIRA: *The Tahoe is on its way to the distillery. V will come get you.*

TEMPERANCE: *Thank you.*

KEIRA: *Your answers will be there too.*

Finally. Ask and you shall receive. Magic.

With newfound determination, I prepare to get on with whatever comes next for me.

Thirty minutes later, I'm in a parking lot I haven't stood in for over a month, staring up at the building that no longer feels like my second home. Shockingly, it's not a lackey standing beside the Tahoe with the keys. It's Mount.

He wastes no time getting to the point.

"With Rafe gone, you're no longer a target. No one should be following you, but just in case, I'll have someone continue to keep tabs on you."

My gaze jerks to his in surprise. "Continue?"

He nods but doesn't explain why he's still having someone watch me. Instead, he cuts to the only thing he clearly cares about. "Don't bring Keira into this again. If you need something, you call me. My number is on the card in the glove compartment."

I give him a nod. "Okay."

"The keys to your warehouse are in there too."

"How did you know about the warehouse?" Shock permeates my tone.

Mount doesn't answer, just turns away as another black car pulls up.

"Take care, Temperance." He slips into the backseat and he's gone.

I watch the car drive out of the fenced parking lot and release a long breath. As much as I want to go inside and give Keira a hug and thank her, I won't. Mount doesn't want me near her, and I can respect that.

Instead, I shoot her a quick text thanking her before checking the back of the Tahoe.

When I see my sculpture inside, my lips stretch into a genuine smile.

I have a long overdue delivery to make.

Valentina's eyes light up when she steps back from the piece and stares at it. "It's incredible. Truly, Temperance. Incredible."

"I'm sorry I'm so late."

She gives me a small smile. "I understand completely. I wasn't going to rush you. I know you've been dealing with . . . well, I wasn't going to rush you."

The pity in her eyes unleashes a new wave of grief, but I keep my composure. Come hell or high water, I'm not going to cry for an hour.

Be happy, I remind myself. *Or at least pretend.*

Maybe if I pretend enough, I'll finally get there. I'm

not sure if happiness falls under the *fake it till you make it* category, but I'm going to try.

I force the corners of my lips upward. "Do you think someone will buy it?"

"Are you serious? I'll have this sold before you drive away. People have been waiting. I shouldn't tell you that, but it's true. After sending a picture and dropping a few lines in the right places, I've been getting calls. I have at least five more buyers interested in large pieces—and they're buyers who aren't afraid to pay."

"How much do you think?" It feels crass to ask, but I need to know.

She gives me a number that's more than what I make at the distillery in several months.

"Really?"

"Yes. So, if you're able to get back to work anytime soon . . ."

"I am," I assure her. "I need to. It'll be good for me."

When I say the words, I realize just how true they are. Having tools in my hand and creating something would be the most therapeutic thing I could do right now. When I thought about burying myself in work before, I felt even more suffocated.

Because I was thinking of the wrong work.

Now that I've been forcibly served another reminder that life is short, there's another item I need to think about adding to my list. And while it's not as scary as the other one I refuse to put on paper, it's still pretty terrifying.

Quit my job.

As much as it sears me with burning anger to admit it, Kane was right about one thing. Working at the distillery isn't what I want to do with my life. It doesn't fill me with joy.

Life is too short to be unhappy, and that includes showing up for work doing something I don't love when I have the opportunity to get paid for my passion.

"Give me a list of everything you think your buyers would want, and I'll get to work. I'll deliver them as soon as they're ready. No more screwing around and taking forever."

"Temperance . . ." Valentina's voice is soft. "You only need to do what you can. Don't run yourself ragged just yet."

Her eyes are kind and I know she's genuinely concerned, but Mount's speech kicked me in the ass. I'm done with self-pity. At least, I'm trying to be.

"This is the best thing for me right now. Please, let me do it."

She studies me and finally nods. "Okay. I'll put a list together and text it to you. Although . . ."

"What?"

Valentina stares at my skyline sculpture for a moment. "How would you feel about having a showing of your own? Not a massive one, but a dozen or so pieces. It's the best way to launch you as an artist in the community, but I know that's a lot to ask. It's not like you can just magic these up."

Her suggestion rocks me, but even in my shock, my first thought isn't *no*. It's *how fast can I make twelve sculptures?*

"Really? You'd do that?"

"Of course. It's not purely altruistic, you realize. I'm making money on these too."

"I know. You should be. I don't know anyone who would buy these. And certainly not for more than I could make in a few months at my day job."

Valentina shoots me another smile, and this one is devoid of any pity. "We got this, girl. You get to work, and I'll start planning as soon as you can give me a ballpark date when you could be ready."

For the first time in over a month, a different emotion bubbles up inside me.

Hope.

SIX
TEMPERANCE

That new feeling of hope lasts for all of three minutes after I leave. Just long enough for me to hear the *thwump-thwump-thwump* of a tire on the Tahoe going flat as I coast toward the side of the road and an empty parking spot.

I stare up at the tan headliner and send a seeking glance skyward.

This is not a sign. This is not a sign. I repeat it to myself over and over until I start to believe it.

I'm a capable woman. *I've got this.*

After I park the Tahoe, I hop out and circle the SUV to see the damage. Rear tire, passenger side.

Not a big deal. I can change a tire.

I crouch down to check the rubber treads for whatever caused the flat, and freeze when I see a half-dozen nails in a grouping no bigger than my fist.

What the hell?

32

This isn't some random flat tire. This was *vandalism*.

In broad daylight.

A creeping sensation, like the one I've felt for the last day, sends a shiver of concern down my spine, but I beat it back. *I'm not going to live in fear.*

Regardless, there's no arguing that someone did this on purpose. Someone wanted me to get a flat tire. I rise to my feet and turn, scanning the street for anyone who may be watching me.

No one stands out.

Not the woman carrying several bags from a shop up the street. Not the man walking his Pomeranian. Not the two kids texting and not watching where they walk.

Finally, my gaze lands on a dark SUV idling in a parking spot at the end of the street I just turned off.

Mount's guy keeping tabs on me?

I stare harder at the blacked-out windshield like I'm suddenly going to be able to see through the limo tint, but it doesn't help.

Either way, I'm done here. I open the passenger door of the Tahoe, yank the keys out of the ignition, grab my purse, and wrap a hand around the edge of the door to slam it closed.

Remembering what Mount said about the keys to the warehouse, I pause.

Do I want them? Do I want anything *from him? From either of them?*

Screw it.

I open the glove compartment and a card falls onto the floorboard. *Mount's card.*

I only pocket it because I don't want to drag Keira into my life if things goes sideways. And besides . . . you never know when you might need to call the devil.

My gaze lands on the set of keys on a leather fob.

Make a decision, Temperance.

I debate leaving them, but if I take them, it still doesn't mean anything. I don't have to go there. I grab the keys and shove them in my purse before locking the Tahoe and striding home with all my senses on high alert.

When I walk into the courtyard, Harriet has white sheets spread out on the grass.

What in the world could she possibly be doing next?

She walks out of her house wearing a black silk caftan that billows behind her, a tray in her hand and a smile on her face.

"Am I interrupting something?"

Her head snaps up like I've disturbed her meditative state, which, knowing Harriet, I might have.

"You're back sooner than I expected. How did it go?"

I glance at the tray in her hand. "Is that paint?"

"Body paint."

She says it like the statement requires no explanation.

"For . . ."

"Immortalizing myself in rainbow color. At least," she glances over her shoulder, "I will be if my gentleman friend arrives to paint me."

"Oh . . . okay. So, this is a good time for me to find somewhere else to go."

Harriet tilts her head to the side. "Only if you have an issue with nudity. My tits may not be as perky as yours, but they're younger than you. My plastic surgeon was a genius in the mid-nineties."

As always, Harriet manages to wrangle a laugh from me.

"How did the gallery go?" she asks.

I tell her about the showing Valentina wants to do.

"That's phenomenal. You're incredibly lucky to have the opportunity. Don't fuck it up."

Her no-nonsense wisdom is always appreciated, as is yet another reminder from her that I could be doing so much more right now than going upstairs and holing up in my apartment.

"I won't."

"Good." She gives me a pointed look. "I'm sure you have better things to do right now than watch two paint-covered septuagenarians fornicate outdoors—like make some art." She glances at her watch. "Actually, you should plan to be gone until at least nine. Maybe ten.

I'm feeling frisky tonight, and he's got the little blue pills."

I glance down at my purse, which holds the keys to the warehouse. The warehouse that holds all the scrap metal Kane had delivered for me.

Can I really face it?

Yes. Yes, I can.

Because I have a list to work on, and not just the one Valentina is going to send me. The list that Harriet forced me to start.

A list Kane would have approved of me making.

Another gut-wrenching slash of pain stabs into me, and I breathe through it.

"I'm not going to ask if you're okay, Temperance," Harriet says to me. "But you will be. You're stronger than you know."

With a decisive nod, I take another deep breath. *I'm stronger than this.*

I look up and meet her concerned gaze. "You're right. I'm not okay, but I will be."

"Good girl."

"I'll just go change and get out of your way."

I climb the stairs, and with each tread, I forge my resolve. *I will be okay.*

As soon as I walk into my apartment, my gaze locks on the crumpled ball of paper I kicked into the fireplace with every intention of burning it, but I haven't yet. The crumpled ball of paper that snapped me out of my haze. The one that wouldn't let me keep pretending I was dreaming this nightmare.

I hate you, Kane. I fucking hate you.

And yet I drop to my hands and knees, reaching into the ashes to retrieve it.

The words blur as I spread it out on the floor, tearing it in several places as I rock back and forth, attempting to fend off the tears that prick at my eyes.

I will not cry for you again. I'm done.

I grit my teeth and focus on the address, memorizing it before pushing off the floor to stand tall with steel in my spine and my chin held high.

I will be okay. Fake it until you make it.

With a deep breath, I head into my room and change my clothes. I'm going to turn trash into dollar bills and buy myself a new life that is so full of everything, I won't have time to think about the hit man who betrayed me and then broke me.

SEVEN

TEMPERANCE

I'm not quite as strong as I hoped. Instead of going to the warehouse with all my newfound strength and emotional armor, I end up on a park bench in front of Saint Louis Cathedral. Not here to pray, but to watch other people *live*.

Tourists stand slack-jawed as a small group of musicians wow them with jazz. A pickpocket sees me watching him and decides to leave a woman's purse untouched. *Rare.* A woman sits at her card table, a burgundy-and-gold cloth spread across it as she waits for the next tourist to sit for a tarot reading.

"You. Come."

I shake my head. "No, thank you."

"I'll read for free."

"Nothing's free in this town," I reply.

"For you. Only now. Your sadness is driving away my customers."

Well, damn. And here I thought I was doing a good job of pretending I was a normal person taking in the atmosphere.

She waves me over again, and it's clear she won't leave me alone.

"Fine." I rise from the bench and eyeball the kid who looks like he'd love to snatch my purse. "Not today, boy."

He glares at me before he disappears.

I sit in the folding chair and stare at the woman. Her skin is dark and smooth. Her hair, graying at the temples, is mostly hidden by a beautiful head wrap.

"I'll read for free, and then you'll be less sad and I'll have paying customers again."

"You badgered me into it. Let's do this."

I clutch my purse on my lap as she has me knock the deck and then shuffle it. We split and restack it, and she finally lays out the first card.

Death.

How. Freaking. Appropriate.

I bring my hand to my forehead, but she wags her finger over the table.

"No. This is good."

"Really? Death is a good card?"

"It's change. Transformation. Endings. Beginnings. You need to put the past behind you if you want to embrace your future and the opportunities awaiting you. This is your time. Your time to start anew and leave what was once behind you in favor of what can be."

I gulp down the lump in my throat as she talks about sudden and unexpected change. Being caught in a tidal wave I feel like I can't escape. The need to leave emotional baggage behind.

When she finally stops, she waits in silence for me to meet her gaze. "You can go now."

"Wait. What? That's it?" I jerk my chin down to look at the card again before glancing back up at her.

"You only needed one card. You already know what you have to do. You're not a stupid girl. You have plenty of life left to live. Go do it."

I stumble out of the chair and rise.

"You didn't believe. Now you do. My job here is done. Feel free to tip for my services."

This woman . . . I don't even know what to say to her. She saw right through me to the heart of things. I could say she just read my body language while I was on the bench, but she didn't stack that deck.

I fish a twenty from my purse and lay it on the table. "Thank you."

She inclines her head regally, and I walk away from the table shell-shocked.

As if I needed another sign.

Tomorrow. Tomorrow I'll go to the warehouse and start getting on with my life.

EIGHT
TEMPERANCE

The next morning, I leave my apartment and smile when I see the body-painted sheets flapping in the breeze. Thankfully, I stayed away long enough for Harriet to finish, and avoided seeing her and her gentleman friend.

My resolve almost falters when I make it to the road and wave down a cab, but I remind myself I have more than one pressing reason to go to the warehouse—my Bronco is locked inside, the Tahoe is at a tire shop because apparently *all* of them needed replacing, and I'm sick of not having a vehicle.

I'm not touching any of the other cars or SUVs, though, I promise myself as the cab driver brings us closer and closer to the dot on the map on my phone.

When we reach the nearest cross street, I knock on the divider.

"Let me out here."

He brakes to a stop, then looks back at me and the largely unoccupied buildings around us. "You sure? This don't look safe, lady."

He's probably right, but something feels wrong about having him drop me off directly in front of it.

I don't know why I care about keeping the location a secret from some random cab driver, but I do. Maybe because it was kept a secret from me for so long.

Besides, a text to Mount confirmed that it's his man in a dark SUV that's been following the cab since I got in it. Which means I have at least a thin layer of security.

"It's fine."

I cringe as I say the word. *Fine*. I hate it. It's always full of shit. No one actually means they're fine or something is fine when they say it. But today, I'm determined to be one step closer to whatever the hell *fine* really means.

"Your funeral," he says as I shove cash through the Plexiglas divider.

The word *funeral* hits me like a cheap shot.

"Thanks a lot," I mumble as I climb out and look down at the map on my phone as he drives away. I should be staring at the route, but all I can see in my mind's eye is my brother's casket being slid into a vault at the mausoleum. It took a decent chunk of my payment from that first sculpture I sold to Valentina to pay for everything, but regardless of how badly Rafe had screwed up in this life, he deserved to be honored in death.

Blinking back tears, I force myself to walk in the direction of the warehouse.

The dark SUV idles slowly behind me as I walk. *Super covert.* I snort-laugh to myself because it's better than giving in to the tears that want to slip down my cheeks.

With every footstep, I brace myself for what's coming next.

I can do this.

It's just a building. That's all it is. A pile of bricks and steel beams full of metal and lies.

I grit my teeth and keep pushing forward. When I stop in front of what appears to be the right building on the map—one with no address—I approach the door.

This could be it. I look over my shoulder at the SUV as it pulls into the parking lot of the building across the street.

What the hell does that mean? That I'm at the wrong build-ing? Or that whoever is driving doesn't want to draw attention by being parked in front of the right one?

My temper flares as I reach into my pocket and pull out the keys. I jab one into the lock and it slides home.

I steady myself before turning it. The bolt slides. With all my courage shored up, I twist the handle . . . and it doesn't budge.

"Are you fucking kidding me!" I kick the door with one of my steel-toed work boots and instantly regret it as pain shoots up my leg.

"How the hell am I supposed to get in then, huh?" I yell the question to the universe, wanting to punch something next, but not dumb enough—or male enough —to do it.

That's when I spot the box. It's dark blue and it matches the overhead garage door. There's a padlock on it, but no place to insert a key.

Great. Super-spy technology for the super-secretive hit man.

Fuck you, Kane. Every time I say his name, even in my head, another spike feels like it's been jammed through my belly.

I'm not saying his name anymore. I'm done.

I grasp the padlock between my thumb and index finger. As I twist it from side to side, the shank opens.

"What the hell?" I unhook it from the box and look down at the flat front. *It's a fingerprint reader.* And it *knows my fingerprint.*

He planned this too.

The knowledge is another fist to the gut that almost doubles me over.

He knew I'd come here without him. I bury the tears and betrayal and open the box to find a keypad.

Fucking great. Like I know some magic combination to get inside.

I don't even know his goddamned birthday.

More pain.

Blindly, I punch in the only thing I can think of—my birthday.

The fucking overhead door moves. A single tear tracks down my cheek as more well in my eyes, blinding me to the beautiful cars inside as I slam the cover closed and relock it.

It takes everything I have to walk inside.

One foot in front of the other. Right. Left. Right. Left.

I have one destination in mind. The control box to lower the door and lock myself inside.

When the door touches the floor, I finally allow myself to breathe.

Mistake.

The familiar scent of motor oil, brake dust, and exhaust fills my nostrils, and a pang of longing hits me hard enough to make my knees wobble.

By force of will alone, I stay upright.

I scan the bodies of the four-wheel drives I was in lust with before, and realize I was wrong.

I can't do this.

Not today.

Not even a little bit.

I need to get in my Bronco and get the hell out of here as fast as I possibly can before I lose all the ground I've gained.

My Bronco is parked facing the overhead door on

the opposite side of the warehouse. I sprint for it, ignoring the fact that I'm losing the battle with my tears. One after another, they hit the floor as I dodge mirrors and bumpers.

I wrap my hand around the door handle and yank it open, climbing inside like I'm being chased by snarling wolves . . . *or memories I can't face.*

I throw myself into the seat and close my eyes, congratulating myself on a narrow escape from letting him break me again.

Until I open my eyes and see a piece of paper on the passenger seat with familiar bold handwriting.

I'm sorry. It had to be this way.

Agony tears through me like the ragged edges of metal.

"Don't you fucking apologize to me, you coward! How dare you apologize to me!" My scream echoes through the whole warehouse.

I grab the piece of paper, crumpling it in my hand, and shove the door open again.

"You don't get to apologize for lying to me over and over again and *killing my fucking brother*!"

As I scream like a woman possessed by demons she'll never escape, that moment my world ends comes rushing back in vivid clarity.

One month and a few days earlier

One moment Kane's hand is empty, and the next, he's holding a gun and it's pointed at Rafe.

He pulls the trigger.

Chaos explodes as a deafening shot echoes in the lobby of the airport. Everything goes quiet in my mind when I see Rafe grab his chest, a look of shock on his face as the fabric of his suit darkens with blood.

I can't hear myself screaming.

I can't hear anything.

Another gunshot shatters every dream I had for the future as my brother's body jerks again before he collapses, lifeless, on the carpet.

I can't believe what I'm seeing.

Blood. So much blood. Everywhere.

"No!" I scream, jerking my head to look at Kane, but his face is expressionless. *This isn't happening. This can't be happening. I'm making this up.*

Someone tackles me to the floor just before another shot rings out and pain explodes in my head. With my cheek pressed to the carpet, my vision goes blurry as another body hits the floor beside me.

Kane.

No longer expressionless, Kane's face is contorted with agony. He clutches his chest the same way Rafe did, and his eyes roll back in his head.

His lips move, and I swear he utters two words.

"I'm sorry."

Another wave of anguish rips through me as I watch the man I love die.

"No! This can't be real! Kane can't die!" My lips move, but I don't make a sound.

When everything goes black, I don't care if I ever wake up again.

NINE
KANE

About eight weeks earlier

Ransom started a fucking shit show all because of pussy. It always comes back to pussy. I told him to steer clear of Magnolia Maison. Tangling with her is about as smart as carrying around a black widow on your shoulder like a fucking parrot.

Actually, a black mamba would be more accurate. Her history is littered with the dead bodies of men who thought they could tame her.

Ransom might have actually had a chance, because I'm pretty fucking sure she's hooked on him, and yet somehow, she still managed to drag him into the line of fire. And now his sister is in the crosshairs.

Fuck you, Ransom.

The woman asleep in my bed will not pay for her brother's bad judgment. Not while I'm still breathing.

But I can't tell him how fucking pissed I am at him until I can get in contact with him. Right now, my messages on the dark web aren't being answered.

I'm guessing that wherever he is, he doesn't have an internet connection. Even if he did, the man barely checks his regular email, let alone the dark web.

Ransom works old school—through word of mouth and referrals. Generally, he only takes jobs he knows are solid from clients who won't end up fucking him over.

But then you introduce the most powerful drug in the world—pussy. That's why we're in this situation.

I pull out my phone and call Magnolia. She doesn't answer until the fourth ring.

"This better be important."

"You think I'd fucking bother you if it wasn't?"

"I'll hang up if you cop an attitude with me, *Saxon*."

Magnolia knows me by my alias, and she knows what I do. Shows just how bold she is that she doesn't care. Or maybe she just knows I won't take out a woman.

She's right. I have lines I won't cross, and that's one of them.

"You hear from him?" I don't have to tell her who I'm talking about.

"Not since he said he was going dark."

"You get any other information on what we're dealing with? There's gotta be a good fucking reason he wouldn't deliver on time."

She goes quiet on the other end of the line.

"You better tell me every goddamned thing you know right now, Magnolia."

"It's bad. Real bad." Her voice is a whisper. For a woman who's seen what Magnolia Maison has seen— and done what she's done—to say something's *real bad*, it has to be *really fucking bad*.

"Tell me."

"I didn't know." She sounds like she's choking it out.

"Fucking tell me."

"They're running human cargo." Shame drips from her words as my blood turns to ice.

"*Fuck.*" I rise from my chair and grip the back of my neck with my free hand. "Tell me you're fucking kidding me."

"I wish I could. I didn't know. I would never have hooked him up with the job if I'd known. You know—"

"I don't know shit, woman. You sell pussy. Why the fuck should I think you'd stop short of human trafficking?"

There are some people I truly fucking hate in this world, and one category would be human traffickers. Scum of the earth, and every single one of them deserves the fate they subject others to.

"I didn't know! I would never. You have to believe me. I've *been* sold. I wouldn't do that to someone I hate, let alone someone I've never met. Please, Saxon. You have to help me fix this."

I tilt my head back to stare at the beams above me. "This is fucked, and you know it. Ransom wasn't gonna smuggle people. You set him up for this. Was that the plan? Did you want him dead?"

"No! I love him!"

"Jesus fucking Christ. Like I believe you."

"Then don't believe me. Just find him before they do."

I almost tell her that the people she hooked him up with are already paying me a half million to bring him in dead or alive, but I don't. Magnolia can't be trusted. She's proven that.

Instead, I say, "Call me if you find out anything at all. You understand me?"

"Only if you do the same."

"Agreed." I hang up the phone with the lie still hanging in the air, knowing I'll have to deal with her sooner or later, but I can always hope for later.

Because right now, this entire fucking game has changed. Magnolia set Ransom up to traffic human cargo, and that explains why they want him dead.

He didn't deliver. He won't be delivering. Knowing Ransom, he's already let every single one of those poor fucks go with cash in hand to make their own way in the world.

And in doing it, he left himself and his sister wide open.

I glance up at the monitor to the left and fix my gaze on the spill of dark hair on the pillow as Temperance curls toward my side of the bed.

How the hell am I going to climb between those

sheets and breathe in the sweet scent of her skin and be able to fall sleep, knowing she'll never be safe until I put them all in the ground?

I can't.

I need a plan.

Neither she nor Ransom will ever breathe easy while a single person involved in this mess lives to order them dead.

I can't believe Ransom would run now, though. He has to know they'll come for her if he does. He might have questionable morals, but he's not a complete piece of shit. The fact that he wouldn't deliver human cargo is proof enough of that. There's no way he'd let his sister pay for his mistake.

No, he knows I'm covering his ass. We made a deal a long fucking time ago. If anything ever happened to me, he'd cover my mom, and if anything ever happened to him, I'd watch over his sister.

Well, Ransom, I'm watching over her. I just didn't plan on getting hooked on her.

I never should have touched her at the club. As soon as she walked through the door, I knew it was some kind of setup, but watching the unholy temptation that was Temperance Ransom made me not give a shit. I was willing to take the risk because I can handle whatever anyone throws at me. Now, if I had to put money on who set it up, I know exactly where I'd put it.

On Magnolia.

One more reason I don't trust her. She always has a

hidden motive, and now I'm starting to see it. She wanted me with Temperance because she knew I'd move heaven and hell to save her brother.

After a few more moments of watching Temperance sleep, I tear my gaze away from the monitor. I have more work to do before the sun rises.

TEN
KANE

About five weeks earlier

S eeing Temperance in jeans and an old T-shirt, with her hair up in a bandana and her hand on the throttle of the airboat, is a hundred times more devastating than watching her work in those sexy little skirts and blouses.

This woman truly doesn't realize what she brings to the table. She's beautiful, but not afraid to get her hands dirty. She's a hard worker, but rarely lets anyone see just how brilliant she is. It didn't take me long to realize she's the whole fucking package.

And what the hell am I supposed to do with that information?

I'm withholding more from her than I'm telling, but keeping her in the dark is the best way to keep her safe. And right now, that's all that matters. That's all I can let matter.

The thought of anyone trying to extract information from Temperance—or putting a single mark on her skin—sends me into a rage strong enough to tear this boat in half. I would do anything to protect her. *Anything*.

She sends us skidding around another bend in the bayou, and against all odds, I smile. It's not something I did much before I met her, but Temperance brings it out of me.

She backs off the throttle for a beat and points. "There. Up ahead. See it?"

My head swivels in the direction she indicates, and I reach for the .45 tucked in the back of my jeans. It fits in my hand like I was born to hold it, and maybe I was.

Maybe I was born to hold Temperance Ransom too.

I push the thought away. Right now, I don't know what the fuck kind of trap her brother might have rigged here.

He's a bayou boy through and through, and it wouldn't surprise me to find he's got World War II claymore mines rigged to trees to blow our fucking heads off.

"Approach slowly," I tell her, and she gives the boat just enough gas to keep it moving forward.

"It's not like they won't hear us coming."

"That's not what I'm worried about." I raise the gun in front of me, ready to pick off anyone who might have gotten here before us.

"Don't shoot my brother."

"If he shoots first, I make no promises."

I say it, but I don't need to. Ransom isn't going to be here. There's no way. Not with how fucking loud this boat is and how easily Temperance was able to find it. Ransom knows his ass is on the line, which means he's going to be somewhere a hell of a lot harder to find. I don't want to tell his sister that, because crushing her budding hope feels too cruel.

Toughen your ass up, Savage.

I shake my head, but she doesn't see. When it comes to Temperance, I'll never be tough. And that's probably what's going to get me killed.

We search the cabin, discovering a note in some gibberish only Temperance can read.

Don't look for me.

Like that's going to happen, you fucking dick.

Ransom isn't naive enough to think what he did doesn't have consequences. The scent of cooked food hangs in the air, so he hasn't been gone long. I don't need to touch the ash in the metal fire pit to know it won't be ice cold.

Now I just need to wait for Temperance to turn her back on me for a moment, which she does as she walks toward the door of the cabin, admitting defeat.

It still amazes me she'll turn her back on a hit man. But she doesn't see me as that man. I never want her to see me as that man.

I crouch next to the woodpile and see a scrap of paper. A note from Ransom.

Shit got fucked. Laying low. Don't fail me now.

I shove it in my pocket and tuck a burner phone into the bundle of wood. There's only one number programmed on it, so there's no question of who he needs to call. As soon as he turns it on, he'll see a text waiting.

Plan has changed.

Three words that are going to change all our lives.

Now all I can do is hope like hell that Ransom gets it and calls me, or we're all fucked.

ELEVEN
KANE

Hours later, after we return from the swamp and finally leave that motherfucker Elijah's warehouse, I'm in my command center with my heart still beating like the war drums of my ancestors.

I watched him watching her.

I watched him *wanting* her.

But what made me rage?

Watching him make her fucking *question herself*.

Elijah may have let her go like a noble son of a bitch once, but I could read it in his every move—he wouldn't let her go again if she ever gave him another chance.

I hate that he's making me face the question I've been putting off.

Will I be able to let her go?

I glance up at the monitor to see Temperance sitting at my kitchen counter, working on her laptop.

I like seeing her in my space. I like seeing her *period*.

Could I handle seeing her with another man?

Before I can answer the question, one of my secure lines rings, and I tense.

Ransom.

I answer. "You hear us today?"

"What the fuck are you doing letting my sister poke around the swamp? What if they'd been there? You're supposed to be keeping her safe, you piece of shit. Keep her locked up in a safe house and sit on her."

"Nothing happened," I say, because I can't tell him that I would die before I'd let anything hurt her.

"I don't fucking like it."

"Then maybe you shouldn't have taken a fucking job trafficking *human cargo.*"

Ransom goes quiet. "I didn't know. I swear to fuck, I didn't know. You know I wouldn't."

"But you did, and now your sister's ass is on the line too."

"You think I don't fucking know that? You think I don't want to hand you my bowie knife to gut me for doing this? I fucked up. I fucked up bad, but I'm not gonna let this touch her. You have to promise me this doesn't touch her." Desperation rings in his tone.

"There's only one way I can promise that."

"Tell me!"

I glance up at the monitor and watch as Temperance surveys the contents of my fridge.

She's going to fucking hate me for the rest of her life. I squeeze my eyes shut.

"What? Tell me!"

I can live with her hating me forever, as long as she lives. That's the only thing that matters.

"You have to die, Ransom. And I'm going to be the one to kill you."

TWELVE
KANE

I'm going to lose her. There's no question about that. The only thing I haven't figured out yet is how soon.

Ransom agreed to my plan, and now my life is like the sand draining in an hourglass. The closer I come to the end, the sooner Temperance will be safe.

I could spend the rest of the time we have left being pissed off because I finally found the woman who could handle the life I live, only to lose her just as quickly.

Or . . . I can make every single second of it count.

I'm choosing the latter.

I know it's the selfish choice when the screams of my name echo off the rock walls of the basement room at the club. The club that brought us together.

It should only be fitting that the woman I suspect of putting this entire mess in motion confronts us as we leave Haven.

I can almost empathize with how frantic Magnolia

is, *until* she tells Temperance exactly what kind of cargo Ransom was smuggling. Now I want to fucking strangle her.

"Was that really fucking necessary? Does that make you feel better?"

Temperance looks up at me, her eyes begging me to tell her Magnolia's lying. "Is it true?"

No matter how pissed off at Ransom I am for putting us all in this position, I hate seeing Temperance's heart breaking. I try to soften the blow any way I can. *Fucking Magnolia.*

"It's true. And I'm sure that's why he couldn't finish the job. He couldn't live with himself if he did. Your brother has lines too. We all do."

"I can't believe he would . . ."

"Believe it," Magnolia says, "because he did. But now someone has to tell me what the hell is happening. Where did he go? If he ran, I'm going with him."

It takes everything I have not to tell her that she's never going to see him again, but I lock myself down.

"Can we please go?" Temperance sounds broken, and there's nothing I want to do more than get her the fuck out of here.

"What? You can't stomach the thought of things your brother does to pay the bills? Feeling a little high-and-mighty since you got that fancy paying job from Ke-Ke?"

I open my mouth to verbally shred Magnolia, but Temperance speaks first.

"You don't know shit about how I feel right now. And how could you not tell me you were with Rafe? You draw me in here, telling me half-truths and giving me bullshit warnings. What game are you playing, Magnolia?"

"The only game I've ever cared to win at—life."

"Enough," I bark out. "We're done here. I don't know where he is. If I did, I wouldn't tell you. Not here. Not now. Too many ears. Too many eyes. Besides, I don't fucking trust you any further than I can throw you, Magnolia. So you're gonna have to wait while we sort out this mess."

"You son of a bitch—"

"We're done." All I want to do is get Temperance the fuck out of here as fast as possible, but as soon as I open the door, I freeze as a man with a face from my past steps in front of me.

Lewis Giles.

My former stepuncle. The dirty DA who teed up who knows how many innocent people to be sentenced to death row by my stepfather. The stepfather who started me down this path I now walk.

For a moment, I wonder if he'll recognize me before I remember that not even my own mother would after the plastic surgery I've had.

Blood roars in my ears, drowning out everything as Magnolia steps up beside me to speak with Giles. He extends his hand, and I stare down at it. He's fucking insane if he thinks I'll shake it.

I catch a piece of him saying something about buying an interest in the club because someone sold out, but I'm struggling to keep a tight grip on my control and don't fucking care about anything but getting out of here.

He keeps holding that fucking hand out.

"We're leaving," I say before I get Temperance as far away from him as possible.

With every step I take away from Giles, I can feel his gaze boring into me.

If I believed in omens, I'd say it's a fucking bad one.

THIRTEEN
KANE

After the speed-dating debacle, I can't help but shake my head as I watch the security footage, trying to figure out who the fuck would dare pull a fire alarm at a property connected to Lachlan Mount. It's the man I saw at the bar, and I want to kick my own ass for not getting a picture of him to run through facial recognition.

He has to be connected to the human-trafficking ring. Only someone with balls that big would dare cause a shitstorm on a property protected by Lachlan Mount.

I thought Seven Sinners would have been the safest place for Temperance outside of my warehouse, but apparently, I was wrong.

That means the plan and the timeline need to be moved up. We can't risk letting it drag out.

The knowledge claws at me, and even though I want

to be selfish and keep Temperance with me as long as I possibly can, I know I can't.

I keep watching the footage. Every camera. Every angle. Every frame. I freeze it on an image.

Temperance and me, pressed together after she rushed out of the bathroom. I hit PRINT SCREEN and wait until the picture is done before I snatch it off the printer.

I stare down at it.

I wish I could hold her like that forever.

But I can't. Our time is almost up, and then she'll hate me forever.

After I'm done, she'll want to burn every memory of me out of her mind and spit on the ashes. And as much as it guts me to think about it, I know it's the only way.

As I fold the piece of paper and tuck it in my pocket, one of my secure phones buzzes with a new message. It's from the number I gave Ransom.

I'm ready whenever you say. Cargo won't be found.

Fuck. It's almost time.

But at least she'll be safe. She'll live. And that's all that matters.

I tap out a reply.

I'll tell Mount. Be ready to move.

Ransom responds just as quickly.

I'll be ready.

That makes one of us.

FOURTEEN
KANE

I *make her happy.*

That's what Temperance said before she slammed the car door and stomped her way to the warehouse elevator.

I make her happy. She wants me in her life.

She doesn't know there's nothing I want more than to keep making her happy for the rest of her life, but there's no way that can happen unless she gets to *live*.

I can't tell her how I feel . . .

That I want what she wants.

That I've never wanted a future with anyone before.

That I've never loved anyone like I love her.

That not having that future with her will be the only true regret of a life that should be filled with them.

I can't tell her any of this. But I can show her.

I pull out my phone to call in a few favors.

As Temperance hammers her way through my spare parts and then dives into the two pallets of scrap metal I had delivered from a contact, I watch her.

I suppose it comes as no surprise. Watching is what I do.

But this time, I'm thinking dangerous thoughts.

What if I tell her the plan? Maybe there's a way to make this work so she doesn't hate me.

As she welds two pieces of metal together, I wish I could see inside her head to the vision she has there, but I can't.

There's no doubt in my mind that Temperance Ransom is the strongest woman I've ever met. She's been forged in the fires of life and emerged as something unique and beautiful. Somehow, even though she's been hardened, she retained enough softness to care about a man like me.

Maybe even love a man like me.

Which is why I can't tell her.

The best way to protect her is to keep her in the dark. Let her hate me. Let there be no question to anyone watching from the outside that this is one hundred percent real.

Her grief.

Her pain.

It will shred her. It'll shred me too. But I don't have a choice.

I'll do anything to protect her.

Even die for her.

I pull the picture out of my pocket and stare at us together as I make the last calls I need to seal my fate.

FIFTEEN
KANE

I didn't know words could hurt worse than being shot until Temperance looked into my eyes this afternoon in the car and said, "Please don't be noble, Kane. I can't give you up. I won't. Don't ask me to."

I've never been accused of being noble before. It's not part of my job description.

But for Temperance, I will be anything she needs.

When I pull the gun, I see the confusion and then horror on her face as the shots explode in the airport.

Ransom goes down, just like we planned.

Temperance's scream is infinitely more painful than the bullet that hits my vest. The squib pack bursts, and my shirt and suit jacket are soaked in blood.

I go through the motions, needing to make it convincing as I destroy everything Temperance feels for me.

Her eyes are on mine as I hit the carpet and mouth two words. *I'm sorry.*

I watch as she loses consciousness. She probably didn't even feel the prick of the needle when that bastard tackled her too fucking hard. He'll pay for that.

I'm so fucking sorry, princess.

Again, I didn't have a choice. She has to stay unconscious for this part. She can't see anything that will put her in danger. She needs to wake up thinking she saw me murder her brother and then die.

It's the only way.

SIXTEEN

TEMPERANCE

Present day

"**I**'m sorry."

I can still see the words on Kane's lips, just like I can see them on the paper he left in my Bronco.

Because he planned all of this.

Betrayal slices through me again, along with gut-wrenching guilt. *I helped him kill my brother.*

What kind of sister does that? *A stupid one.*

I look down at the crumpled paper in my seat.

I'm sorry. It had to be this way.

"Fuck you, Kane! You don't get to be sorry!" I scream like a woman with nothing to lose as I jump out of my truck and spin around to face the tools. I came here to get the Bronco, but now I have a completely different objective in mind.

I stomp toward the workbench and look for a lighter and gasoline.

I'm going to burn this motherfucker down.

I spot the torch I used to weld the sculpture I was making for him that day my world ended with three gunshots. *Perfect. Fucking poetic.* I scan the expansive space for anything I can use as an accelerant. A red gas can on a shelf on the opposite side of the warehouse stands out like a homing beacon.

"Fuck your apology, Kane. Fuck this warehouse. Fuck everything. I'm done!"

I start toward the gas can, but before I reach it, a large hand closes over my arm.

"I don't think so, princess."

The rage thrumming through my veins dies for a second at that deep voice.

The deep voice that belongs to a dead man.

I'm imagining things. This isn't real.

My gaze darts down to my forearm, and the fingers wrapped around it are flesh and blood. Not those of a ghost.

Those big hands send an avalanche of memories tumbling down, crushing my lungs.

No. It's not possible. He's—

"Temperance—"

He says my name, and I snap out of my momentary

paralysis to whip around to stare up into icy blue eyes that are now as familiar as my own.

My heart slams in my chest as shock floods my system.

Kane.

He's alive.

He's alive.

This isn't possible. I shake my head, trying to break whatever hallucination I've somehow gotten lost in.

He's a ghost. That's the only thing that makes sense.

The hand on my arm grips tighter. It's big and strong and *real.*

"How . . . you—" I can't get out anything coherent as I jerk my gaze back to his face. "I don't understand." My entire body shakes, sending vibrations through my voice.

"I did what I had to do."

His words send a completely new level of rage boiling through me.

"You did what you had to do? You killed my brother!"

My scream ends on a ragged note as I rip my arm from his hold and flail to grab the closest object that can double as a murder weapon. My fingers wrap around a piece of pipe, and I swing it at his head. Kane latches onto it before it can connect, not even wincing at the impact against his palm.

"Temperance—"

"How could you?" My scream echoes through the warehouse, sounding as demented as I feel.

I jerk the pipe back, intending to swing again, but he yanks it out of my grip and sends it flying. It clangs when it hits the concrete floor, and my instincts roar.

I'm going to make him hurt as badly as I have.

I reach for the wrench, but before I can close my hand around it, Kane's thick arms wrap around me, caging me like a straitjacket.

"Let me go!"

"Never." His deep voice rumbles in my ear, and I struggle against him as he holds me tight. "Never, Temperance. I will never fucking let you go. And I swear to Christ, I didn't kill your brother. He's as alive as I am. I promise. I would never fucking hurt anyone you love. *Never.* I'd end my own life first."

I jab an elbow into his gut before his words sink into my brain. I'm still fighting him like a wild thing when I finally comprehend what he's repeating over and over.

Rafe is alive. He's alive. I swear.

"What?" The single word comes out on a ragged breath as his hold loosens.

"He's alive. I swear to God," Kane says. "It was all—"

I spin in the circle of his arms as disbelief wars with soul-burning rage. Kane's icy blue gaze blazes with tortured agony that matches the emotions fueling my wrath. Drip by drip, a fraction of the pain drains away, and my brain spins in a completely new direction.

"You played me?" I stare at him like he told me they were both abducted by aliens. "Are you fucking kidding me?"

"It was the only way."

The admission might as well be a Golden Glove boxer's combo that knocks me on my ass. I barely stay upright as reality pummels me.

They're alive.

Both of them.

Rafe is okay.

Kane isn't dead.

As much as I want to believe every single word of what he's saying to the very depths of my soul, I'm done living on faith. I'm done trusting blindly.

"I don't believe you."

"I swear on——"

Slowly, coldly, I repeat, "I don't care what you swear on. I don't believe you."

A flash of something flickers over Kane's face. I could swear it's pain, but I don't care right now. It's not even a fraction of the torment I've been living with the past month.

His jaw ticks as he watches me. "Temperance, please——"

I want to believe him. I want to believe him more than I want to take my next breath, but I can't be stupid. I can't be naive. *I can't trust him again so easily.*

"You lied to me! Why should I believe a goddamn thing you say? I want proof. Proof of life. Proof that this isn't just one more elaborate scheme to get me to trust you so you can make a half-million dollars by putting a bullet in the only family I have left."

Kane's expression goes blank, then he pulls out a phone and enters a passcode before dialing a number. He taps the command for the call to go to speaker as soon as it starts ringing.

I wait with the most excruciating hope as it rings four times. Just before I give up hope, he answers.

"What the fuck you need? I'm busy."

"Rafe?" My voice shakes as I say my brother's name.

"Saxon? What the fuck?" It's my brother's voice, his tone sharp, but my faith in believing what I see and hear is shattered.

"I made an executive decision. Your sister needs to know you're okay."

Rafe curses before he replies. "Tempe? That you?"

"Yes," I whisper. I rack my brain to think of a question to ask him that no one else would know the answer to, but Rafe's tone changes.

"I didn't want you to find out this way. Saxon shouldn't have—"

I interrupt him. "How old was I the first time I ate catfish?"

"What?"

"I need to know it's really you. I don't trust him." I glance up at Kane. "I don't fucking trust anyone anymore."

"Fuck. I'm sorry, Tempe. So fucking sorry."

Tears blur my vision, but I refuse to let them fall. "Catfish, Rafe. Answer the fucking question."

"You hate catfish. You got something else you need to ask before you believe it's me?"

A ray of hope cuts through the dark skies that have lined my world for a month.

"Where did you hide Daddy's belt?" I whisper, still scared to trust, but able to let that brightness break through a little more each second.

"I burned it with gas from the extra tank for the boat. Well, I tried, but the metal wouldn't melt, so I gave the buckle to you, and you made something out of it after you learned to solder."

I release a ragged breath.

My brother is alive. My entire body starts to shake as my knees give way and I hit the floor. Kane tries to pull me back up, but I bat his hands away.

"You're alive." My voice breaks and tears rush down my face. My sobs turn to heaves. "Why the hell would you let me think you were dead? How could you do that to me?"

Kane drops to his knees beside me, but I wrap both arms around my middle, holding myself together as though I fear I'll shatter any moment.

"I swear we didn't have a choice," Rafe says. "We had to keep you safe. It was the only way we knew they'd believe it."

"Who? Who had to believe it? What are you talking about?"

Kane answers before Rafe can. "The traffickers. We needed them to think Ransom and I were both dead. We had to take the pressure off so we could eliminate them and keep you safe."

My brain works overtime to comprehend what I'm hearing, piecing together their logic, but it still rips me to shreds when I think of how I've been drowning in grief for weeks.

"It was the only way," Rafe says. "I would never put you through this if it wasn't the only way. You know that."

Rationally, I know my brother wouldn't intentionally cause me pain, but I'm not completely rational yet.

"I could've acted. I'm a good actress."

"I'm so sorry, Tempe. I fucked up." Rafe sounds just as destroyed as I feel. "I should never have taken the job. *Never*. I'll never forgive myself for hurting you."

"Where are you?" I whisper. When Rafe doesn't answer, I whip my head toward Kane. "Really? More secrets?"

"It's safer this way," my brother says.

"No. No more fucking secrets. I'm done with them. Done with all of it. I deserve to know."

"Tell her, Ransom." Kane joins the conversation again.

After a pause, Rafe answers. "I'm hunting down the last threat. Then we can live free and easy again."

My blood, which was finally simmering rather than boiling, goes ice cold.

"You're hunting a human trafficker who wanted you dead?" I jerk my chin toward Kane. "Why didn't you go? You're the killer for hire."

Kane's lips flatten, but Rafe is the one to reply.

"It's my mess, Tempe. Saxon helped more than I deserved. I started this, and now it's time for me to end it."

"Please tell me this isn't some kind of suicide mission. Please tell me you're coming back to me. I can't get you back only to lose you again. Don't do that to me. Not now." My voice cracks and another wave of tears trails down my cheeks. I wipe them away, but I can't help being an emotional basket case right now. I'm entitled after this roller coaster of a month.

"I'm coming back. I swear it on Mama's grave."

The ice in my veins warms a few degrees.

"You better mean that, because if anything happens to you, I swear I'll find you, bring you back to life, and then kill you myself for putting me through hell. You understand me, Rafe Ransom?"

My brother chuckles into the phone. "It's a deal. I gotta go, Tempe. I'll be hugging you in person soon. I'm so fucking sorry for all of this. I'll make it up to you. Don't be too hard on Saxon. He saved my ass. I'd be dead for real if he hadn't thought this whole plan up. Love you, girl."

He ends the call with my echoing *I love you* hanging in the air.

I push off my feet and stumble toward a wall. Kane's large form comes toward me, and I wave him off. I'm not ready to deal with him yet.

"I wanted to tell you . . . but this was the only way."

"Bullshit!" I explode. "It wasn't the only way." I drag my gaze up to meet his.

Kane opens his mouth to speak and then closes it again.

"You *lied* to me. You made me think . . ." I don't even want to say it again. "How could you do that to me? I've been one step up from a corpse for a goddamned month because you couldn't trust me enough to tell me *anything*."

"Temperance—" He steps toward me, and I hold up a hand to keep him back.

"All you had to do was tell me."

His fists clench at his sides as another stream of tears sneaks down my cheeks.

"It had to look real."

"Well, fucking great. I'm so glad it looked *real* for you. And guess what? *This is real too.* How much I fucking hate you for this is real! How dare you?" I'm shrieking and I don't care at all. I've been through hell, and I told myself I was to blame for every single moment of it. "You made me think *I betrayed my brother and got him killed!*"

Kane squeezes his eyes shut and dips his chin before drawing in a breath and staring me down. "You can hate me for the rest of your life, and I'd still do it all the same again."

I suck in a breath. "You fucking—"

He interrupts me with a roar. "Because now, you get to *live*! *That* is the only fucking reason I did any of it. For you. Because I love you."

SEVENTEEN

TEMPERANCE

The rough brick scrapes my back through my T-shirt as Kane's booming voice echoes in the cavernous building. He closes the distance between us before I have a chance to process his words.

Not just words . . . it's a declaration that carries more power than an atomic bomb. It levels me, burning away all the anger and grief that have ravaged me for every waking minute of every day since I woke up thinking both he and Rafe were dead.

Kane's palm presses against the wall beside my head as he stares down at me, his nostrils flaring and the vein in his temple throbbing.

"I'm sorry. So fucking sorry. I'd rather take a bullet than watch you cry another goddamned tear." He reaches out, and rather than slap his hands away like I would have done only moments ago, I let him catch my tears on his thumbs and cup my face. "Please don't cry."

"You love me?"

His palm cradles my cheek as he studies my face. "Since the first time I watched you pick up a welding torch and I saw the real you. Not the show you put on for the world." His eyes shut for a moment before his gaze bores into mine again. "I told myself I could let you go because it'd be safer than trying to keep you with me. That once this whole thing was over and it was safe, I'd leave the choice of what happened next up to you."

If I thought my emotions were chaotic before, they're nothing compared to the uprising being staged in my brain by the thunderous beat of my heart.

"You were going to let me go?"

He looks away before replying. "I didn't think there was any possible way you wouldn't hate me when this was over. I told myself I'd say good-bye and fade into the shadows, and let you have the life you were meant to have."

"Without you," I whisper.

"Yes."

Kane was right when he said that love and hate are two sides of the same coin. Because even though minutes ago I wanted to kill him, now I can't imagine what he's describing—not having him with me.

I've already lived through that, and it nearly killed me.

His blue eyes burn with emotion. "You have to know . . . there isn't a goddamned thing I wouldn't do to keep you safe. You can hate me if you need to, but that will never change the fact that I love you."

I let his words soothe the torn pieces of my soul, and breathe in his scent. As much as I want to curl up against him and be thankful he's back, I need him to promise me something before I can begin to trust him again.

Kane and I lock eyes. "I can't live with the secrets anymore. I won't. If you can't promise me you'll never lie to me again, I will walk away from you right now and never look back."

EIGHTEEN
KANE

I had a choice, and I made it. I'll live with the consequences because they were worth it to ensure her safety. There's *nothing* I wouldn't do to keep Temperance safe, and I'll never apologize for that. For hurting her, absolutely. I'll never forget the tortured look in her eyes. It'll haunt me for the rest of my life.

I don't deserve her forgiveness, but I want it.

I don't deserve *her* at all. But that doesn't stop me from wanting her more than I want my next breath.

Now, I'm so fucking close to having everything I never knew I always wanted and needed in my life, and all I have to do is promise to never lie to her again. I'd rather cut off my own arm than ever see again the kind of pain on her face as when she walked into this warehouse.

I vow to myself right then that I will find a way to protect her without ever putting her through that kind of pain again. I fucked up. I made the wrong decision. I shouldn't have kept it from her. At the time, it seemed like the safest choice, but after a month without her, I know it was the wrong one.

For the last four weeks, I've lived in a hell of my own making. One where I knew she existed, but I couldn't see her or touch her. One where I couldn't dare break my silence because there were too many threats against her.

I begged Mount—something I would have sworn I would never do—to protect her like he would protect his own wife. I offered him *anything*.

It was only after I had his guarantee of her safety that I left town to start hunting down my targets, one by one. Every time I pulled the trigger, I knew I was one step closer to this moment. The moment when I could come back to her.

I told myself even if she hated me and sent me away, I would let her live her life and fade into the background.

But I would never forget this woman who changed everything.

From Mexico to Canada, I eliminated man after man, until the only one who was left was the head of the trafficking operation. The one they called Lagarto. *Lizard*.

Ransom called dibs on the man who put the price on his head, and I agreed. The motherfucker was wily as shit, leading us both down dead ends to try to find him.

Ransom and I agreed I would come back to New Orleans and track him down from here so I could be closer to Temperance if he tried to make a move on her now that his crew was all mysteriously missing. Not a single one of those bodies will ever be found.

He had to know we were coming for him, and we won't stop until we put a bullet in his head.

That was yesterday.

I've been here less than twenty-four hours, and I already had to stop myself from approaching Temperance a handful of times. All I could do is watch as she squared her shoulders and went on with a life that didn't include me.

It was a new kind of a hell. One I'd never before experienced. And now she wants me to promise I'll never lie to her, or she walks away.

My answer requires no thought.

"I promise. No more secrets. If I'm trying to protect you, I'll do it another way."

I can feel the tension dissipate as her body relaxes against me.

"Thank God," she whispers.

Before I can reply, Temperance wraps one hand around the back of my head and yanks my lips down to hers.

My only thought mirrors her words.
Thank God.

NINETEEN
TEMPERANCE

Kane locks one arm around my back and cradles my chin, tilting my head to take the kiss deeper.

Yes. This is what I need. Him.

Maybe to reassure myself that he's really alive.

Maybe to burn away the remains of the pain I felt from losing him.

Maybe because I love him, and living without him was the most hopeless feeling I've ever faced.

Whatever the reason, I need it desperately.

Madly.

Violently.

Kane's hand shifts to my ass, and I dig my nails into his shoulder, moaning into the kiss.

"I missed you so fucking much." He growls against my mouth as I wrap my leg around his hip and press myself against the growing bulge in his jeans.

"I missed you too."

He pulls back an inch, his blue eyes blazing. "Even when you hated me?"

"Even then, I still would've traded everything I have for one more day with you."

"Thank fuck." His fingers tunnel into my hair, gripping, and I revel in the bite of pain because it reminds me that we're both *alive*.

I wrap my other leg around him and shimmy up his body until we're pressed together everywhere that matters.

Crushing my mouth to his, I try to tell him everything without words. That I need him in the most basic way imaginable. That I missed the taste of his kiss. The hard muscles of his body. His capable hands. The careful, yet effortless way he handles me, giving me what I want and need.

He's the only man who has ever evoked such strong emotions in me. With him, I feel all the extremes. There's nothing average about what we have.

I should have known from the first night when I couldn't walk out of that room, even though he was a complete stranger, that this—*us*—would change my entire life.

Sometimes your body recognizes things before your mind. I don't know why it took me so long to see it, but now, I'm getting out of my head. I'm following my instincts, and my instincts tell me that regardless of everything that has happened, Kane is *mine*.

I buck my hips against him, and Kane's grip tightens. He backs me up to a section of the stainless-steel workbench I'd scrubbed clean the last time I worked here.

As soon as my ass connects with the flat surface, I release my grip on his neck to yank at the hem of his T-shirt. Kane helps me with one hand until the fabric no longer stands in my way.

I'm not letting anything stand in my way anymore when it comes to Kane, not myself or him.

This is happening. *We* are happening.

My instincts from before were right—what makes me happy is standing right in front of me.

I marvel at him like I've never seen him before. His heavily muscled shoulders, covered in ink that wraps down his arms. The beautiful wings and heart that spread across his chest.

This man, this work of art, loves me.

The realization is still shocking, but I hold it close. I'm never letting the memory of him saying it for the first time fade.

My fingers trail down his hot skin until I reach the button of his worn jeans, but he distracts me by tugging at the T-shirt I'm wearing and pulling it up and over my head.

"Need to see you. Need to feel you. Fucking missed you so goddamn much." Kane's voice is raw, and I feel his need in every brush of his fingertips over my skin.

His fingers find the clasp of my bra and free me

from it. When he moves in, I press my chest to his, needing the contact. Soaking up his heat.

"I missed you so much." My words are just as raw as his.

"Never again, princess. Never. Again."

His vow unleashes a new torrent of need inside me.

"Hurry. Please."

His gaze snaps to mine. "Only if I get to savor you next time."

"Deal."

It's like someone fired a starting pistol. We both launch into action, tearing at each other's clothes until I'm naked on the workbench. But I can barely feel the cool metal against my ass because my body is burning like a fever.

As soon as he kicks off his shoes and jeans, he nudges his heavy cock against my slick entrance. "I love you, Temperance. No matter what happens, I will never stop loving you."

With that declaration, he pushes inside, and there's no hope of me staying silent. His name falls from my lips and echoes in the warehouse.

"Yes!"

He's buried to the hilt, and my nails dig into his shoulders as he begins to pull back.

"Not yet." There's something I need to say to him before I lose my mind with pleasure.

Because I've never needed a man to feel complete, but I can't argue how strong and beautiful I feel with

Kane. I could have lived without him, but I never want to. And that, I believe, makes all the difference in the world.

His gaze finds mine.

"I love you too," I tell him, and it's as if a wave of relief washes over his body.

He glances up toward the metal beams above us. "Thank God."

When he meets my gaze again, I see everything he feels for me reflected in his blue eyes.

"I need you."

My words unleash a category five hurricane. Kane is a force of nature as he pulls back before pounding into me, over and over, finding my clit and wringing orgasm after orgasm from me.

He won't stop, even though I'm not sure I can handle another climax. But he doesn't slow. He doesn't relent.

My screams echo in the warehouse as I take everything he gives me, and give back just as much.

When he roars and I shatter one last time, I know the truth.

I'm never letting him go. No matter what.

Kane is mine.

TWENTY
KANE

C ontentment is a feeling that has eluded me my entire life. I've lived in solitude, never truly connecting with another human being.

I've never needed company or companionship to keep myself entertained. All it took was a quick trip to the club to watch a scene and get off, or maybe find a stranger for the night that I would never think about again after I walked out the door.

With Temperance, everything has been different from the beginning.

I didn't know I could want or need someone so badly. In the past, I would have worried about whether having a woman of my own could be turned into a weakness that could be exploited. But watching Mount and Keira has shown me that the right woman can make a man even stronger. Even more purposeful and deadly. Because there are no lengths to which he won't go to protect her.

Regardless of what happens next, we will be fine.

It's with that thought I doze off in my bed, my limbs tangled with Temperance's.

We're on top of the world. Not a damn thing or person can come between us.

Or so I think until I wake again.

The side of Temperance's face is pressed to my chest and she shifts, opening her eyes.

"Give me a couple hours, and I'll have the strength to go get your stuff from your apartment and move it here," I say as I absently stroke her hair.

She stills. "What?"

"Your stuff. You're moving in. The warehouse is yours, anyway. Might as well use it. Plus, it has everything you need to work, and I'll get you anything else you want."

She rolls off my chest and props herself up on an elbow. Her dark eyes look too serious.

"What's wrong?"

"We need to talk about a few things first."

"Like?"

"The fact that I don't want to move out of my apartment again so you can keep me locked away from the world until you deem the threat has been eliminated."

My thoughts had been exactly that. "I won't compromise on your safety. You can't expect me to."

"Then I guess you're moving in with me, because

I've decided that I'm going to *live* for real this time, which means not being shut away from the world."

Fuck. Of course she would want that, and I'm not going to stand in her way . . . but with one stipulation.

"I can't move in with you. What will your friends think? The guy who killed your brother and came back from the dead? That's not going to happen."

"First, did I ask you to move in with me?" She tilts her head.

"Temperance—"

She interrupts me with a laugh and a smile. "I'm kidding. I *am* asking you to move in with me, and you don't have to worry about the rest."

"What do you mean?"

"I didn't tell anyone anything."

I blink at her several times. "What?"

The humor fades from her eyes. "I wasn't exactly functioning, and even if I had been, I wasn't going to tell everyone how stupid I'd been. Keira said she didn't know who you were. So, I assume that means only Mount does, which means . . . you *can* move in with me. You can have a life outside the shadows too, Kane."

The realization stuns me.

A life outside the shadows. That's not something I've ever tried. Keeping to myself was always the easiest solution, and everything else presented too many problems to deal with.

But for Temperance, I would find a way to solve every single one of them. I wouldn't have to watch her live, I could do it with her. It was like someone handed me the keys to a kingdom I never contemplated entering before.

"Okay." The word sounds rough, but so are my emotions.

She smiles. "You can also have the warehouse back. And the cars. I don't want them."

I think of how I watched her start for the gas can in her anger and pain. "You were going to burn it down."

She nods. "So let's agree that you need to take it all back."

"If lighting this entire place up was going to make you feel better for even a second, I would've let you."

Her smile disappears. "It wouldn't have made me feel any better. Probably worse."

"I know, princess. That's why I stopped you."

Her eyebrows go up. "Not because you wanted to save the cars?"

"They don't mean a damn thing compared to you."

Her face softens, and she leans against me once more.

"How about I make you a deal? I keep the cars here, and you and I both work here. But when you're done, we go back to your apartment at night."

Temperance's eyes go wide. "You'd do that?"

"Mount's the only person who knows I was the one who shot your brother. The witnesses would describe the disguise."

"Yes. Good."

"And even if that weren't the case, I'd find a way to make it work. Because, apparently, you haven't gotten the message yet that I'd do anything for you."

She presses a kiss to my chest. "Thank you."

"But I need you to do one thing for me."

"What's that?" she asks, once again finding my gaze.

"Tell me you love me again."

When she said those words, it felt like my heart was going to explode. No one has told me they love me in over fifteen years, and to get those words from Temperance, with all the promise in her eyes, was a miracle.

"I love you, Kane . . ." Her lips flatten as she trails off.

"What?"

"I don't know your real last name. Can I know it?"

Only two people know that Kane Savage is still alive, and giving that information to Temperance is also handing her the keys to bringing down everything I've built.

Considering I'd hand her a gun to put a bullet in my head if she asked, it's not a tough question to answer.

"Savage. Kane Savage."

Her eyebrows shoot up. "Seriously?"

I nod.

"Your name is Savage?"

"Formerly Sergeant Kane Savage of the United States Army."

"That's a good name. A strong name."

"My father was army too. Didn't make it home from Vietnam."

"I'm so sorry." Temperance's expression turns introspective.

"Thank you."

Her mouth moves like she's debating how to ask another question but can't find the right words.

"You can ask me anything." When I say it, I'm surprised to find I mean it completely. Whatever Temperance wants to know, I'll tell her. I'm done keeping secrets.

"How did this all start? What you do? I know that's not part of the army sniper program. Or is it? Do you work for the government still?"

"It's a long story."

"Do you have somewhere to be?"

"Nowhere but with you." That's also the honest truth, so I start at the beginning and tell her about my past.

An hour later, Temperance is staring at me, dumbfounded. "You did this all for your mom? To keep her safe?"

I swallow the lump in my throat that always crops up whenever I think of Ma. I've kept close tabs on her over the years through the one person I trust who knows I'm alive—Jeremiah Prather, the owner of Bulletproof, and the one who probably saved my life by calling Mount in —but it's not the same.

"If you want to get down to it, yes. I loved being a

soldier. It was a good life. I loved it. Gave me purpose and a cause. Knowing that I was doing what I did for the greater good. I didn't care that I could make a better living by pulling the trigger for different reasons."

She cuddles into my side. "Do you wish you were still in the army? That you'd never walked this path?"

I tighten my arm around her and stroke her arm. "No. Because then I wouldn't have you."

TWENTY-ONE
TEMPERANCE

I'm still full of warmth and happiness the next afternoon when we finally make our way back to my apartment. As I lock my Bronco, I realize I haven't exactly prepared him for my eccentric landlady.

"Shit," I whisper.

"What?" Kane asks.

"I have a landlady. She's . . . different. To say the least. She doesn't know much, but she knows I met a guy at the club, so we need a plan for how to introduce you. Who you want me to introduce you as."

"Use the name we did at the distillery. I used it with enough people that it's the smartest choice."

"So you're going to be Ken Sax to everyone we meet?"

Something dark passes over Kane's features, and I wonder if he's thinking about how his stepfather's actions and his reactions to them stole not just his life from him, but essentially took his entire identity. It must be incredibly hard to never use your real name, so I'm doubly glad he trusted me enough to tell me. He will always be Kane Savage to me, and no one else, regardless of what I need to call him in public.

"For now."

I want to ask what his answer means, but decide this isn't the time or the place. As we walk toward the gate that leads from the sidewalk into the courtyard, questions form in my brain.

Is Kane going to try to reclaim his life? His stepfather is dead, but he never said what happened to his dirty DA of a stepuncle or the crooked sheriff.

I'll save those questions for later.

When we stop in front of the gate and I fish out my keys, I glance over at the small sculpture Kane's holding that I made this morning for Harriet. It's a small thank-you for her constant support—not only over the last month, but for as long as I've known her.

I think she's going to like the man and woman I welded together in what is undoubtedly an erotic pose. Anyone else might think this piece is inappropriate to give a seventy-something-year-old woman, but Harriet is special.

Although, now that I think about it, I'm a little terrified what kind of conversation this piece is going to evoke with having Kane there. I'm used to Harriet's outspoken nature, but Kane . . .

"I really do need to warn you—"

"Temperance? Is that you, darling?" Harriet calls from the courtyard, her voice carrying through the brick pathway leading into it.

And . . . my chance for warnings is over.

"Yes. I brought a friend with me."

I add that last bit because one of the few times I brought my brother here, Harriet was skinny-dipping in the small splash pool and had to quickly grab a robe after Rafe and I both saw things we'll never be able to forget. And then we had the body painting she was doing more recently . . . and before both of those times, there was a gentleman friend I once saw *way* too much of.

"Don't worry. I'm decent. Mostly."

With the gate clanging behind us, we walk into the courtyard. Harriet is wearing a lemon-yellow silk caftan, and it's clear she's gotten out of the pool recently.

"How was your swim?" I ask.

"Lovely, but not nearly as lovely as this man with you. A gift for me? He's quite delicious," Harriet says.

I choke on the spit in my mouth, sputtering, but Kane is way ahead of me.

"It's a pleasure to meet you, ma'am, and while Temperance does have a gift for you, I'm not it. She's the only woman for me."

Harriet presses a hand to her chest like she might swoon, and I grip my purse tighter because I might too.

"Oh, I like you. Come closer."

Kane steps toward her, and Harriet shows no shame as she inspects him from head to toe.

"Yes, I approve." She looks to me. "Temperance, where did you find this fine man? Did you put him on your bucket list? If so, I need to go get a piece of paper and put in an order with the universe, because I've not yet had the pleasure of so much muscle and ink and *rawr*."

I'm slightly mortified by Harriet's claw-like motion and lioness roar, but Kane's laughter booms in the courtyard.

"Thank you, ma'am. I'm sure the universe will be happy to grant your wish."

"Now, where's this present you mentioned?" Harriet asks, her gaze landing on the sculpture in Kane's hands. "Is that it? Did you finally make me one? I'm not above begging shamelessly because I've been dying to beg, but didn't want to pressure you. I should've pressured you. If that's not mine, I will beg." Harriet's tone gets more insistent with each word, and I want to kick myself for not making something for her sooner.

I take it from Kane and hold it out to her. "Of course it's yours. Long overdue, I know."

She takes it from my hands and holds it like it's a priceless piece of art, and I hope someday it will be.

"It's beautiful." Her tone is hushed as she turns it, inspecting all the small, intricate pieces I welded together to form the bodies. "Absolutely breathtaking. I'll treasure it, as soon as I get done rubbing it in the face of all my friends that I have a Temperance Ransom original."

A Temperance Ransom original. That doesn't sound too bad. Actually, it sounds freaking incredible, and that's *before* Harriet keeps talking.

"One of my friends snapped up one of the pieces you sold through Noble Art, and she's been rubbing it in all of our faces. I wanted to tell you, but you weren't ready to hear it. Now you are." She pins me with a wise stare. "Go make some more, because you're going to make a damned fortune, girl."

"I will," I say, blinking back the stray tears burning behind my eyes.

"How did your boss take it when you told her you were quitting?" Harriet's tone is conversational as she sets the sculpture on the table next to her glass of wine. Her question assumes I've done the thing I haven't quite worked up to doing.

"Uh, I haven't actually quit yet."

Beside me, Kane squeezes my hand.

"What are you waiting for?"

"Guts?"

Harriet laughs. "Girl, you've got more guts than anyone I've ever met. Now, take your man upstairs and try not to break the bed or fall through the floor. But tomorrow, you go tell that boss of yours that she needs to replace you on a permanent basis."

It might sound like Harriet is giving me orders, but she's only reinforcing what I already know I need to do next. It's time. I decided that when I was at Noble Art.

Lord, was that only two days ago? It feels like a lifetime. Maybe because my entire life has changed since then. I'm no longer alone in the world, fighting feelings of guilt, grief, and betrayal.

Now I have the man I love beside me, his promise to never keep secrets from me again, and my brother is somewhere working to end this and get back home to where I can slap him upside the head and then hug him.

Even with the little bit of fear I still have churning in my gut about Rafe hunting down a human trafficker, I feel better than I have in over a month.

All because of the man beside me.

Am I crazy to put so much faith in him so quickly? I refuse to think so. I see the way Kane looks at me. With everyone else, he might hide his truth, but he's letting it shine with me.

He loves me, and he's going to keep the promise he made.

There are certain things you just *know*.

We leave Harriet after twenty minutes of listening to her incredible stories and make our way up to my apartment. I forgot how small it is until Kane is looming over me, filling the tiny space with not only his body but his presence.

I glance at him. "We need a bigger bed, don't we?"

TWENTY-TWO

KANE

Temperance and I are both introspective as she drives to Seven Sinners, fighting morning rush-hour traffic in the Bronco. The passenger seat isn't my normal spot, but Temperance needs to feel in control of her life. After everything I threw at her, I understand why she needs it, and I can give that to her. Hell, I'd give her anything. My blood. A kidney. An arm.

She's already got my heart, and I never want it back.

I love you hasn't exactly been part of my vocabulary in a long time. I've only said it to one other woman on the planet, and she doesn't even know I'm alive.

These past few weeks, after my second "death," I've thought a lot about Ma, and how much I'd like to see her again up close and not through binoculars or in pictures taken by Jeremiah. I'd like to tell her she still has a son. She's not alone. That I love her, and the only reason I disappeared was for *her*. To give her a chance at a happy life, even if it didn't include me.

But with Giles still alive . . . it's not safe. He's seen my face now. If he heard about a man matching my description visiting Ma, he wouldn't hesitate to dig into my background and try to figure out who I am.

Do I think he'd be successful? *No.* I've paid a fuck-ton of money to cover my tracks. But am I going to risk Ma's safety if there's even a remote chance that this could blow back on her? *No way in hell.*

Which means I keep my distance, regardless of what I want. It would be stupid to do anything else.

If only someone would put out a hit on Giles, things might be different. But no one has, and unlike in the situation surrounding Ransom, I'm not about to embark on vigilante justice when it comes to Giles. There are too many risks for only my own selfish reward.

When Temperance pulls into the blacktopped parking lot in front of the tall brick building that houses Seven Sinners distillery, she parks around the side, near the other employees' cars. I'm sure it's out of habit, one she's about to break.

I assume that's the reason for her silence—coming to terms with the fact that she's leaving the job that has been the driving force behind her ambition for years.

"You okay?" I ask her as she turns off the SUV.

With a deep breath, she turns to me. "I think so. I know I need to do this."

"Only if it's what you want."

"You told me I need to do it."

I reach out and lay a hand on her thigh. "Because I saw how different you are when you talked about your art versus working here. There's nothing wrong with this job. If you loved it and wanted to keep it, I'd be one hundred percent for it. But since you don't seem to want to split your time anymore, I say go after the one that gets you closest to your dream."

She nods. "I just . . . I'm worried about how Keira is going to react. She's done so much for me, and now I feel like I'm letting her down."

Ah. So that's it.

"You did the job you were hired to do, and now you found something else you can make a living at and enjoy more. There's nothing wrong with that."

"Okay. I can do this."

I lean over and press a kiss to her cheek. "You can do anything, princess. This was just a stepping-stone in your path. It's your boss's dream, not yours. She'll understand."

She pauses with her hand on the door and her front teeth digging into her lower lip.

"What?"

"Mount told me to keep my mess away from Keira, or he'd take care of me."

I reach out and take her hand. "You let me worry about Mount. Besides, if that was what he said, then he'll approve of this move."

With another deep breath, Temperance opens the door of the Bronco. "Wish me luck."

TWENTY-THREE
TEMPERANCE

The familiar smells and sounds of the distillery greet me as I step inside the building. I catch sight of the back of Louis Artesian's head as he steps into a storeroom.

The walk to Keira's office has never seemed shorter. *Shouldn't it take longer to get there?*

I wipe my sweaty palms on my black pencil skirt before adjusting my yellow blouse again.

I picked a sunny color thinking it felt optimistic and cheerful, but it's not helping. I've halfway convinced myself to turn around so I can change into jeans and a T-shirt and go hammer metal instead.

Why am I afraid to tell her?

Because Keira's been there for me for years. Working at Seven Sinners was the best job I've ever had in my life, along with giving me a reliable income and carrying some prestige, so it seems insane for me to quit. And yet, I can't make myself come back and work here.

Giving up the steady paycheck is the biggest risk, but the new theme in my life seems to be taking chances. And this morning, I'm taking one of my biggest chances yet.

At least, the biggest one outside of telling Kane that I loved him.

I shake my head at the wonderment of that. Not only is he *not* dead, but he *loves me* and we have a future now.

I pause in front of Keira's closed door and tap on the wood.

"Who is it?" she calls out.

"Temperance," I reply.

"Come on in."

My hand slips off the handle on the first try, but I get it on the second and twist. As soon as I step inside the office, I freeze.

Keira isn't alone. Mount is here.

Oh fuck.

Immediately, I start to back up. "I'm so sorry. I truly didn't mean to interrupt you. I can come back another time." *Like when I have body armor on,* I add silently.

Mount's black eyes lock onto me, carrying a silent warning not even I could miss.

"Thank the Lord, you're back! I've missed you like crazy, and the work is getting out of control, even with the new people we hired."

Before I can answer, Mount speaks for me.

"She's not back. She's here to quit."

His words leave no room for debate. Even if I hadn't come here to give my notice, Mount would have ensured it. I suppose, in some respects, that makes this even easier. He doesn't want me here, and no one questions the king.

"What?" Keira blurts out the word, her shock clear from her tone. "She's not going to—" Keira goes silent and stares at me. I don't know what she's looking for or what she sees on my face, but her expression falls. "You are here to quit, aren't you?"

Stupid tears. They burn behind my eyes, like I haven't had enough emotional turmoil over the past month.

"I'm so sorry, Keira." I glance at Mount and his chin lifts in approval, giving me the wherewithal to continue. "But I don't want to leave you in the lurch if you still really need me."

Keira looks up at Mount, and they have an entire conversation without ever speaking. When she turns her attention back to me, she shakes her head.

"If this is what you need, then that's what needs to happen. That doesn't mean I won't miss you like crazy, but with the extra help we've hired, we'll figure it out. No one will ever quite be able to replace you, though."

"Are you sure?" I'm not certain how to feel about her easy acceptance, but I decide I'm going to be happy that she's okay with it.

Keira stands and walks around Mount to meet me in the middle of her office. "I'm positive. Running this distillery is the dream I've had since I was a little girl. But just because it's my dream doesn't mean it needs to be yours. I'm never going to hold you back or make you feel guilty for leaving to do something else that makes you happy. Do you have a plan?"

I nod. "I do. Valentina is going to hold a showing at Noble Art for my sculptures. I've already sold her two, so I have a cushion to live on even if things fall apart."

"Don't bank on it falling apart. I saw the piece we sold. You have talent." Keira pauses. "You know I want one, right? Can you make one that looks like the Seven Sinners logo? I'll commission it with a deposit and everything. I want to display it in the lobby."

The tears that were burning behind my eyes get the better of me, and one slides down my cheek. "You do?"

"Absolutely. Inspirational and motivational. I'll take it whenever you finish. No deadline. Just tell me how much."

I laugh because it's the only choice other than bursting into thankful sobs. "I'll have to get back to you on a price. I haven't sorted any of that out yet."

"You ran this business like you were born to it. I know you can run your own like a master. Don't doubt yourself, Temperance. You'll be incredible."

"Thank you," I whisper.

"You never have to thank me for anything. You saved my ass more times than I can count. I'm grateful to you. Besides, it's just wonderful to see you smile again."

Her comment brings me back to the present and everything that has happened in the last few days. A couple of mornings ago, I was a grieving, crying disaster. Today, I'm only a bit of a crying mess. But still, I can't tell Keira why that is. I can't tell anyone why that is. At least, not yet.

I glance back at Mount and find him watching me closely. That's when I remember—*he knows.*

He freaking knew all along. I have to bite my tongue to stop myself from asking why he would keep something so massive from me.

Instead, I meet his dark stare with my own, and we have our own silent conversation.

MOUNT: *Say anything about your brother or your hit man to my wife and you'll face the consequences.*

ME: *You're a fucking prick, but I forgive you because the two most important men in my life are* alive. *Suck a dick, though.*

Apparently, silent me is a lot more daring than real me.

"Mount," I say with a nod. "Good to see you."

He inclines his head. "Glad to see you took my words to heart."

"I'm doing my best."

"Keep it up. I'll expect to see the piece Keira wants commissioned in the lobby within the month."

Keira whips around to look at her husband. "Six months. I'm not pressuring her."

"She needs the money, so she'll get it to you sooner."

"He's right. I'll have it to you as soon as I'm able. But it might take longer than a month because of the showing."

My former boss shakes her head at her husband and turns back to me with a wink. "Feel free to send *him* the bill now, but I'll take it whenever you finish."

A small chuckle escapes my throat. "Duly noted."

"I'll have some boxes delivered to your office, and while we pack up your stuff, you're going to tell me about the temp assistant you had while I was on vacation who mysteriously disappeared when you stopped coming in."

My gaze shoots to Mount, and his expression carries a warning I can't ignore.

"He didn't work out as an assistant so much . . . because we started dating. He gave me some space while I was dealing with my grief, and things are . . . going well now."

Mount gives me an approving nod, and Keira beams.

"I'm so happy for you, Temperance. I look forward to meeting him."

I smile too because I feel like I just dodged one of Mount's bullets.

"Now," Keira adds, "let's get you packed up so you can go chase that dream of yours even harder."

———

Forty minutes later, Kane helps me carry the boxes from my Bronco up to my apartment.

"I can't believe I did it. I'm officially unemployed!" I feel lighter, as if a massive weight has been lifted from my shoulders.

I set the small box on the counter as Kane deposits a larger one in the corner of the living area and turns to face me.

"You're *self-employed*. There's a difference."

I take a deep breath, and a wide smile stretches my cheeks until they hurt. "Either way, I feel really good about it. It's like I'm getting a brand-new start at life."

He crosses the room, closing the distance between us with only a couple of steps.

"That's how I felt the second time you came to the club."

Another wave of warmth blooms in my chest. "Really?"

He nods.

"Why the second time?"

"Because the first time was a dream. The second time held a different kind of promise. Like it was the beginning of something that could be more than a club fling. Everything about it was different. *You* were different."

I remember how he left me covered with a blanket, leaving a note saying he wanted to see me again. Knowing that was the absolute truth fills me with another wave of warmth.

I take the opportunity to ask another question that has occupied my mind. "If you hadn't seen me at the distillery during the auction, would you have come looking for me?"

His blue gaze turns solemn. "Of course. You're not the kind of woman a man can walk away from without intending to make his way back to as soon as possible."

Those pesky tears shimmer again, but this time I don't let them fall. I have a better idea.

"Kiss me, Kane."

"You mean kiss the artist I'm in love with?"

My smile widens, because now I can check one of the things off my list. "Yes. Kiss her."

His hand tangles in my hair as he lowers his lips to mine.

While we're curled around each other in bed an hour later, my phone chimes with a text.

"I don't want to look. I don't want reality to intrude today."

Kane sweeps a lock of hair off my face. "We're real,

princess. Reality ain't gonna change anything about that. Go check and see if it's important, and come back to me."

I untangle myself from him with a sigh and head for the living room to find my purse. My phone chimes again.

I pull it out and check the screen. "What the hell?"

"What?" Kane calls out.

"It's Magnolia."

TWENTY-FOUR

KANE

I don't know what the hell Magnolia wants, but I don't like one of the most notorious madams of New Orleans texting my woman or coming to her apartment. Apparently, whatever Magnolia has to say to Temperance, she can't say over the phone or put in writing because it isn't safe.

That makes me even more hesitant to let Temperance face her alone, but I couldn't argue the fact that Magnolia might be more open with her than with both of us.

And this is why I'm listening through a crack in the door from Temperance's bedroom as she lets Magnolia in.

"What's going on? You sounded like this was important," Temperance says.

"You think I'd rush my ass all over the French

Quarter if it's not important? Of course it's important, girl. You done lost your fool mind in grief, haven't you?"

Magnolia stood behind Keira that day at the cemetery when they thought they were burying Ransom, and I have to wonder if Ransom was dumb enough to reach out to Magnolia to tell her the truth about being alive. My guess is no, because I can hear her heels strike the wood planks of Temperance's living room as she paces.

"What are you talking about?"

"You. Quitting your damn job. Grief has you all screwed up. That's the only reason you'd be dumb enough to do it. But you need to go tell Ke-Ke you need it back right the fuck now."

The urgency in Magnolia's tone rubs me the wrong way. She knows something I don't, and that is never a good thing.

"Why?"

Temperance's question is exactly the one I want answered. I have no idea why Magnolia would give a shit about Temperance quitting.

That's when Magnolia drops the bomb.

"Because you need to be in the circle of Mount's protection, girl. There are still people out there who could come after you because of your brother. Unless you want to end up dead."

People? We know about Lagarto, but if what Magnolia is spouting off is true, we missed someone we didn't know about, and that can't stand.

123

TWENTY-FIVE
TEMPERANCE

I stare at Magnolia like she's not speaking English. "Who? What are you talking about?"

The slightly intimidating woman—with her perfect hair, perfect clothes, and perfect makeup—shoots me a cutting look.

"I know you ain't part of my world, and I don't want you to be, but you don't know what a bad fucking move you just made. You put yourself at risk the second word got out you aren't under Mount's protection anymore. You need to get back under his protection, or you're going to end up as dead as your brother."

That answers one question. She doesn't know Rafe is alive.

But she apparently has information that I don't have.

"Who do I need protection from?" I ask, hoping Kane is listening to this conversation word for word through the cracked bedroom door. Whatever Magnolia has to say, we both need to hear it.

"Who do you think?" She cops an attitude, which seems to be her natural state, propping her hand on her hip.

I tap into all the acting skills I don't actually have and dig into my grief, which is still simmering just below the surface. "Kane said . . . Kane said that if they killed Rafe, there would be no reason for them to come after me. I don't understand." My voice breaks at the end.

Magnolia's gaze sharpens. "Who the fuck is Kane?"

Shit! Not only am I a terrible actress, but now I've given away part of Kane's true identity. *Great, Temperance. Just great.*

Part of me expects him to burst through the door from my bedroom any moment, but it doesn't happen. It's up to me to get myself out of this mess and find out what Magnolia knows.

"That's what he told me to call him," I whisper.

"The motherfucker who killed Rafe?" Her voice shifts to a hiss.

I don't answer because I realize I've fucked up royally. But Magnolia doesn't need me to speak because she's got plenty to say.

"I hope the devil welcomed him with open arms, because otherwise I'd kill him myself."

"Who do you think is going to kill me? Why do I need protection?" I ask, trying to redirect the conversation.

Magnolia doesn't ask permission, just moves toward my sofa and takes a seat. "Sit," she orders. I swear, the woman is bossier than Keira.

I follow her direction, but only because she's the keeper of information I need.

"I need to know. I can't protect myself if I don't know."

She presses two fingers into each temple and exhales. Only then can I see the weariness in her expression. Magnolia might be the most beautiful woman in New Orleans, but there's a hard edge to her that has sharpened over the last month, as if honed by grief.

"Mags, please. I didn't ask to be involved in any of this."

Her gaze cuts to mine. "I don't want to explain this to you. You don't need to know the things I know. You don't need to carry the burden."

"But if I'm in danger—"

"That's the only reason I'm telling you this. Figured I'd take it to my grave. Here's hoping confession is good for the soul."

I wait in silence because it sounds like she needs a moment to gather her thoughts before she begins.

"It's my fault. All of it." Magnolia's face creases with pain. "I never should've gotten him involved. I shouldn't have passed the information about the job on to Rafe. Or, at least, I should've asked more questions so he knew what he was dealing with."

"Wait, *you* got him the job with the . . ." I pitch my

voice lower like I'm about to say something awful, which I suppose I am. "Human traffickers?"

A flash of pain lights up Magnolia's expression. "People come to me when they need things, or when they need things done. I use my connections and make things happen. They didn't tell me what the job was, just asked if I knew someone who could take it."

Knowing what little I do about her backstory, I can't imagine Magnolia would ever do such a thing. She'd been on the streets since she was a teenager, and selling other women . . . that's just *wrong*.

"But—"

She waves a hand to silence me. "I know what you're going to say. But Magnolia Maison sells women all the time, so what makes this different?"

I nod.

"Because all my girls make a *choice*. They know what they're doing. I give them alternatives before they take their first john. If they can't stomach doing it, I help them find something else they can do to earn money that doesn't involve spreading their legs."

"How do you have any working girls at all then?" That's a mystery to me. I thought they were all women acting out of desperation.

"You're a smart girl. What would you do if you could make a grand a night, easy, doing one job, or spend all day working to make a hundred? Maybe two hundred if you're lucky? My girls get paid top dollar. You do the math. If you need money and don't have many other options, it doesn't take a genius to see the upside of the proposition." She pauses. "You see where I'm going with this? Plus, I'm under Mount's protection, which means my girls are too. People know he won't stand for girls getting smacked around. It's a fucking death warrant."

I see the picture she's painting, and it's different from the one I expected. But that's not the point of this whole conversation.

"So I'm supposed to believe that you wouldn't traffic women."

"Never."

"And yet my brother got involved in a human-trafficking ring."

"It was a favor for an important man. But I didn't peg him for moving human cargo."

"Another human trafficker? Did my brother know about this guy?" I ask, immediately wondering if there's someone still out there that Kane and Rafe don't know about.

Magnolia shrugs.

"Who?"

This question doesn't come from me, but from Kane as he steps out of my bedroom and into the living room.

Every drop of blood drains from Magnolia's face. When she unfreezes, she crosses herself.

"You're a fucking ghost. I know you're a ghost." Her head whips to me. "What the fuck is going on, Temperance? Why you got a fucking ghost in your apartment *who killed your fucking brother?*"

She tenses on the couch, looking ready to spring into action at any moment—either attacking or running out the door—but I'm stunned by her questions.

How could she possibly know that Kane took the shot to kill Rafe and then was shot and killed? Magnolia wasn't there. The news never reported on the incident at all. Mount covered it up.

So how can she know?

"No ghost, Mags. I'm real, and I want a name. Now." Kane's tone brooks no argument, but Magnolia doesn't seem to hear the threat as clearly as I do.

She vaults off the couch, and before I realize what she's doing, she has a small pistol in her hand, pointed at Kane.

"No!" I spring out of my seat and throw myself in front of him, blocking his body with mine, giving Magnolia my back. I tense, waiting for a bullet to rip through me, but it doesn't come.

"What the fuck are you doing?" Kane grips my shoulders and glares down at me. His blue eyes are as dark as thunderclouds, and his lips are pressed into a hard line.

"I can't let her——"

He grips my shoulders and peels me off the front of his body, exposing himself once more to Magnolia. "You *never* put yourself between me and a bullet. *Never.* My life isn't worth even a second of yours."

"Someone better tell me what's going on right the fuck now." Magnolia's voice shakes, and I glance at her.

The gun is still in her hand, and it trembles in front of her as her finger caresses the trigger.

"How the hell did you hear about what happened at the airport?" Kane asks her.

"Doesn't fucking matter, does it? It especially won't matter when I make sure you're *really* dead instead of just faking it."

"Rafe isn't really dead either." I blurt out the truth, because there's nothing I won't do to get the barrel of that gun away from Kane. "He's alive. I talked to him yesterday. It was a setup."

The barrel wavers. "I don't believe you. But I do believe *Saxon* had no problem collecting the rest of the fee for his hit after he pretended to take a bullet."

"Put the gun down, Mags," Kane says. "There were no real bullets."

All his order does is make her level the pistol on him again.

"You better prove it right the fuck now before I pull this trigger and end you where you stand. I don't miss."

I try another tack. "You think he wouldn't already be dead if Rafe wasn't alive? I would've killed him myself. In fact, I tried before he told me Rafe wasn't dead."

Magnolia's gaze darts from me to Kane and back again.

"You want to talk to Ransom?" Kane asks. "We'll

get him on the phone for you right now, but you gotta put the gun down first."

"You think I'm stupid? This gun doesn't leave my hand until I see his face. And don't think for a second if I pull the trigger, I'm gonna miss. I never do."

She jerks her head at me.

"You get his phone. I don't trust him further than I can see him. And I sure don't trust him not to pull a gun on me for pointing one at you. I recognize the look on his face. I've seen it on Mount's before he orders someone dead for saying something wrong to Ke-Ke."

I meet Kane's gaze, and when he nods, I cross to the bedroom and get his phone. "I need your pass code."

"Your fingerprint works."

My chin jerks in his direction. "What? How is that possible?"

"You really want to discuss that right now?"

I shake my head and press my thumb to the reader. Sure enough, it opens. "We're going to talk about how the hell you made that work later."

"Call your brother before I disarm Magnolia and she accidentally shoots one of us, or a stray bullet hits Harriet."

My gaze goes back to Magnolia, and while she's moved her finger off the trigger, she hasn't lowered the gun.

I nod and ask Kane for the number. He repeats it from memory. Before I can tap to engage the call, Magnolia interrupts.

"No. I want to see his face. I'm not trusting you don't have some actor set up, ready to impersonate him."

Her request actually doesn't sound crazy. I probably should have asked for the same, but it didn't even occur to me.

"Then you need a different number, and I don't know if he'll answer it."

"You better hope he does."

Magnolia's voice is sharp as I dial the new number and then tap the button for a video call. Before it connects, I level a stare on her. "Don't threaten us. Remember what you just told me? *You* got everyone into this. Now they're just cleaning up the mess."

Rafe answers on the third ring. "The fuck you want? You need to see my beautiful face, Saxon?"

I realize he can't see anything but the ceiling right now, so I tilt the phone so my face is in the camera's view.

"Tempe?"

As soon as she hears my brother say my name, Magnolia releases a wild cry.

"Oh my God!" She stumbles toward me, and Kane snatches the pistol from her hand before she makes it two steps. "Let go of me, asshole."

Rafe's brow scrunches. "Magnolia? What the hell is going on?"

"She—"

Before I can explain, Magnolia snatches the phone

from my grip and stares at my brother as tears stream down her face.

"I thought you were dead. Oh sweet fucking Jesus, I thought you were dead."

I've never seen a composed woman fall apart so quickly. Magnolia loves my brother. That's for damn sure.

I'm not sure what to think of that, but it doesn't matter right now because she's spilling everything she knows to Rafe on the phone.

"I didn't mean to get you involved. I didn't know he was running people. This is all my fault. I'm so fucking sorry, baby. Please come home to me."

Kane cuts in. "Magnolia says there's another trafficker. She came to your sister worried shit was going to spill over onto her. Now she won't tell us the name because she wanted to kill me for killing you."

"Who told you about Saxon pulling the trigger, Mags?" my brother asks, and like us, I think he's wondering if Magnolia knows more than she's saying.

"That's not important, baby. What's important is that you come back to me."

My brother's voice softens, and for the first time, I can picture them being together. "Sweetheart, I can't come home to you until all these motherfuckers are dead, so you gotta tell us everything you know. Who else is involved?"

I figure Magnolia would spill everything when Rafe asked her, but strangely, she gets quiet for a few seconds.

"If you don't get him before he finds out I talked, I'm dead. I'm not giving you a name until you promise that you'll get him first."

"You know I wouldn't let anything happen to you," Rafe tells her.

She narrows her gaze as she stares into the phone. "I thought you were murdered by this asshole for his payday! I grieved you. I'm still wearing black. You *know* I can keep my mouth shut, and you could've told me the plan. I wouldn't have said shit to anyone. You could've trusted me."

I can't help but glance at Kane, because Magnolia sounds a lot like I did when I learned the truth. I wonder if my brother's answer will be the same as Kane's was.

"You know I couldn't tell you. I kept you out of the loop for a good reason. I don't want anything blowing back on you. Besides, Saxon and Mount said no way. They were the ones who didn't trust you. Not me."

Well, shit.

Magnolia's venomous glare lands on Kane. "I should've shot you when I had the chance."

"Give us a name, Mags, and you and your man can run off into the sunset together as soon as we kill these bastards."

Her lips purse and her whiskey-colored gaze touches every single person taking part in the conversation before she finally gives up the information.

"Giles. Lewis Giles is the one you need to kill."

TWENTY-SIX
KANE

I fucking knew it.

The only good Giles is a dead Giles. I never had a valid reason to take him out before, but I do now.

"Tell me everything. How far up does this go?"

Giles is a state senator now, so there's not a chance in hell that he's running this alone. If he's trafficking women, then he's passing them along to other buyers who could be in the government too.

"I don't know," Magnolia says, her voice throaty, almost hoarse. "I thought he was running drugs for someone, not people."

"Shit. We got politicians involved?" Ransom asks. "Fucking A. Now we're going to have to take out half the government."

"Please tell me this isn't really happening," Temperance says before looking to me.

These are things I wish I could shield her from, but I

can't. Also, it's time to get a handle on the Magnolia situation. I snatch the phone from her hand and ignore her shout of protest. Keeping an arm outstretched, I block her flailing hands from taking it back.

"You take out your target; I'll dig into Giles and find out who else is connected. I won't take him out until we know exactly how deep this goes. Don't change your objective, Ransom. Got it?"

Ransom nods on the screen. "Got it."

"Find that motherfucker you need to kill and get back here. Apparently, some people give a shit that you're alive."

Temperance laughs, but there's a hysterical edge to it, and Magnolia shouts in agreement, still trying to steal the phone back. I end the call and tuck it in my pocket before stopping her.

"You satisfied? He's alive. He's working to end this. No contact with him until then. Understand me?"

Magnolia practically snarls. "High-handed mother-fucker. Always pegged you as the dominant type, but never as the straight-up asshole." Her gaze flicks to Temperance. "Hope you can handle that."

Temperance steps closer to me and I slide an arm around her waist, pulling her into my side.

"I can handle anything he throws at me."

All I can hope is that she's speaking the truth, because things are going to get uglier before they're done.

TWENTY-SEVEN
TEMPERANCE

Magnolia sweeps out of my apartment with the same dramatic flair as when she came in. As soon as the door shuts behind her, I turn to Kane.

"Do you trust her?"

"As far as I can see her."

His answer doesn't fill me with relief.

"So, what do we do now?"

Kane pulls me in front of him and leans down to press a kiss to my forehead. "We go back to the warehouse."

"We're going to come up with a plan and go nail Giles's ass?"

Kane presses another kiss to my head. "You make art. I dig again for anything I can find on Giles that ties him to this. I have a few contacts on the dark web who might know something. He's been a public figure most of his life, so there are plenty of people who hate him

MEGHAN MARCH

and are willing to sell him out. I just have to find the one with the right information."

I don't like the sound of that, but at least he'll be safe in the bat cave and not out setting up a sniper's nest to take out Giles. *Yet.*

"And then?"

"You let me worry about that."

"Kane . . ." My tone holds a note of warning. "I won't live in the dark. You have to share with me so I don't get blindsided again. That was our deal."

He looks away before he cups my cheek. "I'll tell you as soon as I figure out what the hell is actually going on. Magnolia could have lied. She always has her own agenda." He pauses. "Don't misunderstand me, though. There's no way in hell you're going to be part of anything that goes down. And if it happens quick, you might not know until after it's done."

I don't like the sound of that. "But—"

"Sometimes it happens that way, and there's not shit I can do. But I'll make you one promise—I'm coming home to you no matter what. I've got a reason to live, and nothing will keep me from the life we're gonna have together. Can you live with that?"

"As long as you come home to me."

Two hours later, I've hammered out some of my tension on scrap metal, and I've had flashes of inspiration for several of the dozen pieces Valentina has asked me to create. The one I'm working on now is a much larger version of the piece I made for Harriet. I'm going to have to give her first dibs on it; otherwise, she's going to be devastated. Hopefully, Valentina understands.

As I put my hammer back in its place, it knocks against metal pushed back to the corner of the workbench, between the wall and the toolbox.

The old army jeep I made for Kane. I pick it up and turn it in my hands.

I made it the day my entire world felt like it was shredding apart at the seams. Now, I can tell myself it was blowing up so I could rebuild it bigger and better.

Before, Kane was still mostly a mystery. Even though I was falling for him, I didn't realize how much it was possible to love him.

Knowing that he orchestrated this whole plan with my brother, while it gutted me, showed me that there truly isn't anything he wouldn't do for me. He's put himself on the line over and over—*for me.*

I've forgiven him, but I certainly haven't given him the thanks he deserves. I wrap the jeep in my discarded sweatshirt, tuck it under my arm, and head for the elevator. Once inside, I realize I still have no idea how to get to the second floor.

I hit the CALL button, and wouldn't you know . . . Kane answers.

"You stuck, princess?"

"No. But I think it's time I see the heart of the bat cave."

He chuckles on the other end of the speaker. "Okay."

The elevator starts moving a moment later, and instead of going to the third floor like it normally would, it stops on the second. When the doors open, Kane is there to move the gate and let me out.

I search the space behind him, but it's a simple, dark gray hallway.

"This is it? I was expecting bats and maybe a waterfall."

One of the corners of his mouth tugs up at my joke. "Come on. I'll show you."

He leads me down the hall and stops at the first door before opening it. "This is the gym."

He pulls the door open, and I peek inside.

"Holy shit." My mouth drops open as I survey the massive space filled with equipment. "I was expecting a Bowflex, and you've got an LA Fitness."

Kane laughs, and I soak up the sound.

"Something like that. Come on. That's not the part of the bat cave you really wanted to see."

He's right. I turn to follow him toward another door at the end of a hallway. This one has a fancy-looking keypad and what I hope is a retina scanner. Because that would complete my little mental picture I've been forming of his lair.

And I'm right.

Kane puts his fingers on a piece of glass and looks into the scanner before the door opens—and then my mind is *blown*.

"Holy. Shit. Are you kidding me right now?"

I feel like I just walked into the Pentagon, and not the room for the normal people. This is like the bunker for the joint chiefs and president. Everything looks so fancy, I'm almost scared to touch anything for fear of breaking it.

"Are you staging a nuclear strike from here? Or is that next week?"

Kane laughs again, but I'm not totally joking.

"Not exactly. More like operation *Save Ransom's Ass*."

My humor evaporates, and I'm reminded of why I sought Kane out to begin with.

"I truly can't thank you enough for doing what you're doing. It means more to me than you'll ever know. This isn't anything fancy, and nowhere near enough, but I made it for you and I want you to have it." I hold out my sweatshirt to Kane.

He looks at me with a raised eyebrow. "Your sweatshirt?"

"Inside."

When he unfolds the fabric and looks at the pieces of metal I've welded together, I wonder if he recognizes what it is. My art isn't the kind that you can always tell exactly what I'm trying to portray, but I thought I came pretty close here.

"It's a—"

"Willys jeep," he says, finishing for me. "The kind they used in the army originally, right?"

I nod. "Yeah."

"You made this for me?"

"Before . . . before everything. I didn't have time to give it to you then, but I wanted you to have it now. I truly am grateful."

He holds the jeep in one hand and reaches for me with the other. "I didn't do this for gratitude. I told you, I would've done it even if you hated me. Took me a while to realize that's what love is supposed to be."

"Dammit, don't make me cry again."

"Shh. It'll all be over soon, princess. I promise."

Kane sets the sculpture aside and wraps me in his arms. I breathe in his scent and cling to his strength. We stand there, holding each other for several minutes before I break the silence.

"Is Giles being involved going to make this harder for you?"

I feel Kane's lips press a kiss to my head.

"I don't know. It certainly doesn't uncomplicate it. His connections could go deeper than we realize."

That's what I'm afraid of. "So, what then? Does it mean this will never end?"

Kane's gaze turns flinty. "This will end. I swear it. Even if I have to take out every single person involved myself."

TWENTY-EIGHT
TEMPERANCE

The next two weeks are a strange mix of stressful and surreal.

Stressful, because Lagarto is still running free in Mexico. Rafe had him in his crosshairs outside Mexico City, and the motherfucking Lizard's car blew up just before Rafe pulled the trigger. His bullet took out the nearby window of a store instead. Thankfully, no one realized it wasn't from the explosion; at least, according to the online news article. Lagarto wasn't just slimy, he was slippery too.

I had originally intended to make an alligator for my showing at the gallery, but now any kind of reptile pisses me off.

Instead, I'm creating a sugar skull, and it's going to be *epic*. At least, it will be if I can find something amazing to use for the nose. None of the pieces of metal

I've cut to the shape I want give it the feel it needs. I need something different. Something new.

I pick up my phone and tap Kane's number, even though he's only one floor up.

"Hey, princess. You need me?"

This is the surreal part of the last couple of weeks. Kane and me.

We're forging a new life together, and it's turning out as beautiful as one of my sculptures. It's not perfect or normal, but it's completely ours. We spend most nights at my apartment, in a bigger bed that Kane had delivered, and then in the morning, we get coffee and breakfast at a café before making our way to the warehouse where we go our separate ways to work.

Kane is an avid day trader, something I didn't know until I finally asked what he did to fill his time. It wasn't just money from wet work that paid for this warehouse and everything in it. He's actually a bit of a financial genius, which is pretty freaking cool.

"Yeah, I need to hit a scrap yard."

"And here I thought maybe you wanted to rob a bank."

"I'm laying off the felonies for now, but I need a piece of metal and can't find the right one. I thought maybe a trip to a scrap yard would give me what I need and knock a few more ideas loose." I haven't yet committed to the final pieces I'm making for the showing, and I want to.

"I'm coming down. I know a place you might like."

"Thanks, babe."

I end the call and lay my phone on the workbench before leaning back against it and surveying my work.

In two weeks of solid days spent hammering, cutting, and welding, I've managed to knock out more pieces than I thought possible. And what's more, I'm proud of every single one of them.

I'll be proud to stand in front of them and take ownership of them. Each piece is unique, impossible to replicate. I've made it a point to add an old car part to each one, and I've decided that's my signature.

"Damn, princess." Kane strides toward me, his gaze fixed on the sugar skull. "That's gonna be sick when you're done. It's already awesome."

A smile curves my lips. It's incredible to have the support of someone who believes in you and your dreams. "You think?"

He stops in front of me and brushes a curl back that has slipped free of my bandana. "I know. You're killing it, Temperance. Just like I knew you would. Now you have to talk me out of buying all of them so we can keep them here."

I roll my eyes. "You're not buying any of them."

"I'm not?" He tilts his head to the side. "And why's that?"

"Because you want me to make a huge splash in the art world, and for people to see these pieces in homes all around New Orleans and beg Valentina for more of them so I'm not a one-hit wonder." The last part is courtesy of a small niggling voice that has crept into my subconscious these last two weeks.

"You've already sold more than one piece, so how could you be a one-hit wonder?" Kane asks, confusion creasing his brow.

I glance away for a moment before looking back up. "Only a few, and I went and quit my job on the off chance I can really make a career out of this. What if I can't? What if it was just a few people and a little luck, and after this, no one wants any of my sculptures?"

Kane wraps his arms around me and pulls me against his chest. "Stop. You're not a one-hit wonder. This isn't a flash in the pan. This is real. Your talent is real."

"You have to say that because you love me."

He presses a kiss to my forehead. "It's the truth. You're going to rock the hell out of this showing and have so much demand, you won't know how to keep up with it. I'm already working on sources for more good scrap to prepare for it."

I jerk my head up to stare into his eyes. "You are?"

He nods, and the confidence he has in me feels like the most incredible gift I've ever been given.

He believes in me.

I push up on my tiptoes to brush a kiss across his lips. "I love you so much," I whisper.

"Not as much as I love you." He takes my lips and dominates the kiss.

A bolt of lust shoots through me, and I don't care that I've been working for hours. I need him. *Now.*

Pulling back, I grab Kane's hand and drag him toward a Jeep with no top. It's perfect for what I have in mind.

Kane doesn't argue. No, he helps me strip and then tears at his own clothes.

"Front seat," I say on a groan between devastating kisses. "I want you in the front seat."

"You first." Kane lifts me off my feet and into the passenger seat of the Jeep. Then he climbs in the driver's side, and I step over the gearshift to kneel on either side of him.

"I apologize in advance for what we're about to do to your leather."

"I don't fucking care. All I want is you. Right now." His lips press against my stomach as his fingers find my nipples and tug.

The heat that was already growing between my legs spirals even hotter. I reach for the bar above his head, and he pulls back to watch as I position myself over his cock.

"That pretty pussy's already wet for me?"

"Always."

As I slide down, taking his cock inch by inch, Kane groans. He begins to lift his hips, but I shake my head.

"This is my ride. I'm in charge this time."

Kane's icy eyes flare. "You giving me orders, princess?"

"Damn right, I am."

"You realize that means the next time I come down while you're working, I'm going to bend you over the hood of that Chevelle and spank your sweet ass until you beg me to fuck you."

I grip the bar and begin to move. "You've got yourself a deal."

He shakes his head. "No, what I got myself is the perfect woman, and she's all fucking mine."

A few hours later, Kane holds my hand as we walk down an aisle at a scrap yard, looking for the elusive piece to complete my sugar skull. We've already collected a pallet's worth of metal that we're taking with us, but I still haven't found what I want.

"Do you ever feel like you shouldn't be as happy as you are?" I ask. "Like it's not allowed because . . ."

He stops and tugs at my hand until I face him. "You're allowed to be excited about this showing, no matter where your brother is in the world and what he's doing."

I fix my gaze on the ground. "I just feel guilty that things seem to be going in the right direction for me, and his life . . ."

"His life is where it's at because of him." Kane tips my chin up with two fingers. "You didn't make those choices. He did."

"But——"

Kane shakes his head. "Did he work his ass off to put himself through college?"

"No."

"Did he bust ass to have a respectable job so he could feel good about himself?"

"No."

"Did he pursue a passion that creates something beautiful for the world to see?"

This time I shake my head because the lump growing in my throat makes it hard to speak.

Kane speaks for me. "No. He didn't. He chose his path, and you chose yours. You reap what you sow, Temperance. He might share your blood, but what he does with his life has always been up to him. You couldn't stop him if you tried."

"I know."

"So don't, for one second, let the situation he dragged us all into take away a single moment of your joy for living your dream. *You did that.* You deserve to enjoy it."

Tears, which I should be out of at this point, blur my vision, and I blink them back as I meet Kane's gaze and nod.

When I turn my head, I see it.

The perfect piece of metal.

"There it is," Kane says, but he's talking about the smile tugging at the corners of my lips.

I point behind him. "No, there it is."

As Kane helps me pull out the headlight housing, the excitement that fills me isn't only for the metal I'm using to build my sculpture, but for what *we're* building.

After I pay for the metal and arrange for delivery of the pallet to the warehouse, we turn to leave the scrap yard. Kane's holding the headlight housing as we walk toward the Scout, and I spot a man running toward a dark SUV.

"What the hell?"

Kane's gaze follows mine. "What the fuck is he doing?"

"I have no idea, but . . ." I spot the broken side mirror on the Scout. "That motherfucker."

Kane turns and takes off after him, but the guy is already diving into what looks like a black Tahoe and takes off, tires spinning and throwing gravel.

I rush to the Scout and the first thing I notice, other than the broken mirror, is the divots on the glass.

He tried to break the damn windows. But they're bullet resistant and he wasn't prepared for that.

Kane comes back, not even breathing hard after his sprint, and hands off the piece of metal we found to me.

"The dumbass didn't cover his plate. We're going to track this motherfucker down."

TWENTY-NINE

KANE

The plate belongs to a dead man. *Gregor Standish.* A man that Mount had offered me a contract on, and I said no because I don't shit where I eat.

No self-respecting hit man takes jobs in a town where he has a home if he can avoid it. Have I been unable to avoid it on occasion? Yes. Like the time Mount needed to wipe out an entire cartel contingent. That was for justice, at least in my eyes.

You don't go after a man's woman.

So, why the fuck is a guy driving a dead man's car coming after me?

Unless he's not.

I keep digging into Standish to find out who would want to avenge his death, but all I find is a string of ex-wives who took him to the cleaners.

Before I can keep digging, I get a text from Ransom.

He's arranging another shipment. It's time to end this.

Damn right, it is.

All of this.

I've got a new lease on life, and I'm ready to get to living it without anything hanging over our heads.

THIRTY
TEMPERANCE

S tanding in the middle of Noble Art, even amidst
the chaos of setup, is surreal.

Setup for my showing that is happening *in two days*.

I've taken Kane's words to heart and haven't let my
worries over Rafe's situation detract from my excitement
about what is a dream come true for me. I can still stress
about Rafe and the man he's hunting down, and yet
enjoy this too.

Like right now, I push it all away and let giddiness
sizzle through me like a kid who's just spotted a massive
pile of presents under the Christmas tree.

But this is better than Christmas on every level, even
though it's slightly terrifying. Like facing a firing squad
and hoping the guns shoot confetti instead of bullets.

Valentina's employees bustle around the room,
setting up pedestals for *my* sculptures. I'm supposed to be
helping, but all I can do is stand here dumbfounded,

bubble wrapping clutched in my fists as I watch them treat my work like it's precious art.

Which they think it is.

Insanity.

This is the life I couldn't even have dreamed of. This is the life I wouldn't be living if not for Kane pushing me to go after it. Tears prick the back of my eyes, which seems to be a regular occurrence lately, and I blink them back.

"Pretty crazy, isn't it?" Valentina returns from the back room and hands me a bottle of water.

I accept it and twist off the top, taking a sip for no other reason than it's something to do to distract me from the urge to blubber like a baby over the reality of what I'm seeing.

"I remember the first time I saw an entire wall covered with my paintings, and my name was actually beneath them. It's not something you ever forget."

I stare at the wall ahead of me and the canvases that I know are Valentina's. "You must have been so proud," I say, glancing from the nudes to her face.

"I wanted to throw up, run out of the gallery, and never come back."

"No way. You?" I decide not to mention the fact that I feel like I might need to escape to the restroom and puke in the next five minutes.

She nods. "Absolutely. If you think it's easy to dig something out of the very depths of your soul and then display it in public to be judged by your friends, family, peers, and complete strangers . . . you're insane. This isn't for the faint of heart."

"Thank you for saying that," I whisper. "Because right now I'm mostly excited, but there's this other part of me that wants to puke and then rock in the corner and cry for a week."

Valentina slides an arm around me and squeezes. "You're going to be totally fine. It isn't easy to expose our true self to others, especially those who might not appreciate it. But I can tell you this—if anyone says anything cruel or stupid or hurtful about any of your pieces, that says a lot more about them than it does about you."

My gaze locks on the large piece I did that is a different version of the one I made for Harriet. Nudes, but in metal. Clearly locked in a carnal position.

"I know not everyone is going to like them. Some people will come to throw rocks, literally or figuratively."

Valentina squeezes me again. "Don't waste a minute worrying about them. Bad reviews are as inevitable as the sunrise. Just remember, even Picasso thought everything he ever painted was crap. You're going to do great. If anyone says a cross word to you, chances are Rix will put them in cuffs, and they'll spend the rest of the night dealing with paperwork and lawyers at the police station."

The laugh that bubbles from my lips is genuine, and I send up a prayer of thanks that I've found people like

Valentina in my life who have stepped in and changed its course.

But no one has changed the course more than Kane. And if he heard someone say something bad about my sculptures, I'm pretty sure that someone wouldn't end up in the police station. Maybe the hospital. I'm ruling out the morgue. *For now.*

Today Kane's off chasing down a lead on a human-trafficking shipment and trying to find out if it's connected to the Lagarto shipment Rafe is tracking from his end. Even though I wanted to be involved, it feels good to be doing something that moves us forward, instead of focusing on digging us out of the mess my brother got himself in.

It's been over two months since I've seen Rafe, and that time barely counts because I thought I watched his murder. I've recovered from that. Mostly. But I'm still desperate for a hug and dinner at our favorite restaurant. But until they make sure they cut off the head of the snake—or the lizard—that can't happen.

I haven't seen Magnolia since she left my apartment, and part of me wonders how she's handling this, and if she and my brother are making plans to run off together. Even though I'm not sure whether I should trust her, if she's the woman my brother is in love with, I'm going to welcome her to the family with open arms, regardless of whether she likes it or wants it. That's just the way I am.

Valentina and I stand there in silence, staring at the

sculptures and each lost in our own thoughts, when the front window of the gallery shatters with a crash.

"Oh my God!" Trinity, Valentina's assistant, screams as all three of us instinctively hit the floor.

Tires squeal in the street and we brace, our arms over our heads, waiting for a wash of drive-by bullets to hit.

But they don't come, and the roar of the engine fades away to be replaced by regular street noise.

Valentina tenses beside me. "I have to get to my phone. I have to call Rix."

Her words sound as if they're fueled by the same adrenaline dump that just hit my system. I'm poised and ready to fight for my life, if necessary. I don't trust that the threat is gone just because a car drove away. I have to call Kane.

That's when it hits me—*this has to be connected to me.* I brought this on the gallery. I put Valentina and Trinity in danger. My stomach twists into a knot, and now I think I really am going to vomit.

"Val? Is it safe? What do we do?" Trinity asks with urgency coating the fear in her voice.

Valentina stares at something on the floor, and my gaze snaps to it.

It looks like . . . *a pipe?*

What the hell?

"Trinity, go to the back room. Stay there until I tell you to come out," Valentina says with the tone of authority. "I'm calling Rix. Someone is going to pay for this."

I open my mouth to tell her it could be because of me, but snap it shut. I can't tell her anything.

I have to cancel the showing. It's too selfish to take the chance. I should have never agreed. Lagarto has to know that either Rafe or someone who knew him is alive and hunting him, because his entire organization has been wiped out.

Then logic kicks in. *But . . .* if it was a human trafficker seeking revenge, wouldn't they have taken me or killed us all to prove a point? He wouldn't have just broken a window with a pipe. *Right?*

Then I remember the man at the scrap yard . . .

This is connected to me. I know it.

Now, what the hell am I going to do about it?

An hour later, behind a boarded-up window, Rix looks from me to Valentina and back at the security footage from the cameras he had installed for situations just like this.

I texted Kane, and he responded a few minutes ago that he's on his way. I'm hoping we have this figured out before he gets here, because whoever threatened my safety will definitely fall into the *needs killing* category, and I don't know how to balance that situation while I'm standing next to a cop.

"Do you recognize this prick?" he asks as Valentina leans closer over his shoulder.

I watch as he replays the tape again, studying the thin man who hurls the thick metal pipe through the window.

"He looks familiar," I say. "I've seen him before." I squint at the screen, ninety-nine percent certain it's the guy from the scrap yard, but I don't want to say until Kane gives me the all-clear.

"Or you've seen him a hundred times since we've replayed the video over and over," Trinity says.

Valentina claps her hands. "Wait. I know who he is. Shit. I *know*. That little douchebag . . . How could I forget him?"

"Who?" Rix asks. "Because the last time someone put a brick through your window . . ."

"We all know that was my fault, so let's not dwell," Trinity says.

Valentina reaches out to squeeze the girl's fingers. "Don't worry about that. Because these two things aren't related at all. *That*," she points at the screen, "is Gregor Standish's assistant. Protégé. Or whatever the hell you call the man's hanger-on."

As soon as she says the name Gregor Standish, my stomach drops to my feet. *Fuck.* I knew it.

"Are you sure?" I ask, my gaze locked on Valentina.

"Positive. He came in a few months ago complaining that we didn't have any Standish pieces in the gallery, and that made us *subpar* and *without vision*. Then he tried to get me to take a sculpture on consignment, and was adamant that I price it at two hundred thousand and not a penny less. I told him to take a hike."

"Why in the fuck would he be throwing a pipe through your window now?" Rix asks. "Wait, Standish . . . isn't he the artist who killed himself?"

I bite my lip because I know there's no way in hell Standish's death was a suicide.

Valentina answers his question. "Yes. His pieces were ugly-as-hell modern art. He was supposed to have one auctioned off at the Seven Sinners benefit . . ." She looks at me. "But yours went up in its place."

Heat burns my face and my throat until there's barely room to breathe. As much as I want to tell her what I know and even more, what I suspect, we're standing in front of a cop, and I'm not stupid. I won't say a damn thing that implicates Mount.

Rix's gaze locks on me. "You know something about this?"

I attempt to wipe any guilt from my expression, but it's nearly impossible. I've carried plenty of guilt about the situation along with me for months. The knowledge has been eating at me that if Standish's artwork hadn't been accidentally switched with mine, he'd still be alive . . . and I wouldn't have this dream of an opportunity.

"Temperance?" Rix prompts me when the silence stretches awkwardly long.

I have to say something. Anything. Because with each moment I stall, I sound guiltier and guiltier, even though my only crime is withholding my suspicions— that Mount had him killed for his smear campaign against the distillery, which upset Keira. And I know for certain that Mount would kill men for less than what Standish did.

"Standish was pissed that my sculpture was accidentally auctioned off under his name, like Valentina said," I tell him.

"And?" Rix asks.

"And nothing. I never spoke to him again after we argued about it. He died shortly after."

Rix's pale, silvery eyes bore into me like he's digging for the truth and can see directly inside my brain and soul. "Have you had any other issues that could be related to this?"

My brain reels. So much shit has happened lately in my life that I don't know what is connected to what, but I can't tell him anything without potentially jeopardizing Rafe or Kane.

I hate keeping secrets, but I have no choice. I keep my answers short and pointed. "I didn't know he had an assistant or protégé."

"Could he be out for revenge?" Trinity asks. "I mean . . . if your stuff got auctioned off in his place and he was upset enough to kill himself, that seems like a motive for revenge. At least, on TV it would be."

Rix studies me longer. "Do you know anything else about Standish's suicide? Anything that would make this guy want revenge?"

From the knowledge in his silver gaze, he knows that Keira is connected to Mount, and there's a chance that suicide could have been murder. Even so, there's no way in hell I'm going to confirm that, because even I don't know for sure. And I don't want to.

Valentina elbows him. "Babe, instead of interrogating my newest featured artist, why don't you go out and arrest the guy who threw a pipe through my window and interrogate him. He's the criminal here."

Rix rises from the desk and looks from me to Valentina. "If there's anything you're not telling me, I need to know now, Temperance."

I shake my head and tell myself I'm not lying because there's literally nothing I know about Standish's assistant. I didn't even know he existed until this moment, so I'm not lying when I reply.

"I don't know anything about this guy." I glance at the shattered glass. "Except that if he's after me, then I'm going to be footing the bill for the new window as an apology."

"You'll do no such thing," Valentina says, her tone decisive. "That's what insurance is for, anyway. Although, with two days to go before the showing . . ."

Rix leans down and presses a kiss to her forehead. "Don't worry, duchess. I've already got someone coming to replace it tomorrow. I had the measurements from last time it happened. The show will go on."

THIRTY-ONE

KANE

No one threatens my woman and lives to tell about it.

I feel that to the very depths of whatever is left of my soul. And that's why it's ten times harder to watch Temperance walk into a police station to face this motherfucker when I want to handle things my way.

I should have dug deeper into Standish's life than his ex-wives. I didn't realize he had an assistant who was fucking crazy. I could have prevented this, and I *didn't*. I feel like I've failed her.

My vigilance will know no bounds from here on out.

I wanted to take care of the situation, but Temperance argued that the police needed to sort it out. It took everything I had not to ignore her request. What sealed it?

When she said, "I don't want you to carry around

this burden because of me, Kane. I want to brighten your life, not add to the shadows."

She meant the burden on my conscience for another death. I've never had someone care about the effects of my job on me or my soul before, but Temperance continues to amaze me.

She loves me.

I still can't believe it sometimes.

Instead of shaking her for being stubborn, I held her tight and thanked God again for sending her into my path.

I don't deserve her. But I'm not giving her up.

Temperance Ransom is mine, and she's staying mine until there's not a single beat of my heart pounding in my chest.

I watch as her brown ponytail disappears inside the front door of the precinct. Wearing sunglasses and a baseball cap, I sink lower in the driver's seat of a blacked-out Cadillac CTS-V across the street, impatient and aggravated as I wait.

This isn't the life I want for us—her having to face things alone because I'm a fucking dead man. *Literally.* I should be beside her, and I could have been, but as *Ken Sax.* Not as Kane Savage.

I punch the steering wheel before I pull my shit together and turn up the volume on the transmitter she agreed to carry inside. If I can't be there in person, I'm going to hear every damn word that's spoken. If anyone says a single cross word to her, dead man or not, I'll find a way to get her out of there and so far away that the cops will never find her.

After the pipe went through the gallery window, my digging finally connected the dots. I recognized the assistant's photo. He's the asshole I saw sitting at the bar of Seven Sinners during the speed-dating event, and had to have been the one to pull the fire alarm.

I should have put it together earlier. That's what I do. But I didn't this time because we had too many other things to worry about—namely, keeping Temperance safe while I faked two deaths and then kept *that* from her while Ransom and I systematically removed every person who presented a threat to their safety.

Or almost every person. That Lagarto motherfucker and Giles are still walking the earth, and that's not okay with me.

Giles is only breathing because I still can't link him to any of the trafficking. All I have to go on is Magnolia's word, and that I don't trust. I've been watching Giles for years, and his shit is tight. I don't know what he's doing, but whoever he hired to clean up his tracks is better than I am. But that doesn't mean they won't miss something eventually. I could take him out on Magnolia's word, but my finger doesn't pull a trigger without feeling completely certain, and I'm not sure yet that she doesn't have a hidden agenda—like getting him out of her way at the club.

And then there's Lagarto. About to move another shipment, and well versed at staying off the radar. In the only photo I've been able to find of him, he's wearing a big floppy hat and baggy clothes, which is completely fucking useless. Information about him is the only thing standing between us and ending this, and we need more of it so we can all move on with our lives.

Except . . . Ransom and I don't have lives anymore. We're both legally dead, and while that's never bothered me before, now it does.

It never occurred to me that someday I'd want a woman to take my name. *My name.* Not an alias. Hell, I never thought I'd find a woman I'd want for more than a night.

Temperance changed everything.

My earpiece crackles to life, interrupting that train of thought.

"Ms. Ransom, Mrs. Hendrix. Thank you for coming in today. We know this isn't how you wanted to spend your afternoon, and I promise we'll be brief."

"Whatever you need, Mac. You know that."

Valentina's tone and her use of the cop's nickname tells me she's met the person interviewing them before, and it makes me feel marginally better that they're not working with a stranger. Then again, with her husband being a cop, there's no way in hell he would have let that happen either. I don't know much about Beauregard "Rix" Hendrix, but he doesn't seem like a complete asshole.

"I just want to ask you a few questions about your relationship with Mr. Riddel."

"Who?" Temperance asks.

"The man who's being held on charges of destruction of property and vandalism. This man."

I can picture the cop flashing a mug shot at her.

"I've never met him before," Temperance says.

"But he seems to know you, Ms. Ransom," the detective replies.

"How?" Temperance's question holds a cautious tone.

"He says that you stole his boss's career and caused his death, which, on the books is a suicide. However, Mr. Riddel states emphatically that Mr. Standish's death was the result of a conspiracy to commit murder."

Rix's voice cuts in. "Mac, are you fucking serious with this?"

I'm so fucking glad he didn't send our women into questioning by themselves. Apparently, he doesn't give a shit about breaking police protocol, which I respect.

"I bring my woman and her girl in for you to ask some questions about a broken fucking window, and you want to talk about some crazy-ass theories of the man who did it? He's screwing with you." Rix's reply is barely contained rage, and Mac doesn't have a chance to respond before Rix starts again. "He wants to make sure you're so busy chasing your own goddamn tail that you don't even look at him for what he did. Valentina is pressing charges. End of story."

"Rix, you know I have to—"

"Not listen to petty criminals looking for some

reason why life got them down and they aren't responsible for what they did. Now, take their statements, and let us all get on with our fucking day."

I decide right then that I'm sending Valentina's cop husband a box of doughnuts tomorrow.

Mac relents. "Fine. We have a witness who saw him throw the pipe. She should be in to identify him already. If she confirms it was him, everyone can go about their day."

They chat a few minutes longer before someone knocks on the door.

"Mac, I got something you're gonna want to see," a new voice says.

"What?" Mac asks.

"Suspect went off during the lineup. Got real interesting."

"Send the footage to my laptop."

"You should already have it."

"Thanks." I hear some noise that must be Mac fucking around with his computer. "I'll just watch this and come back."

"Bullshit, Mac. Just play it," Rix says.

"Fine. Not my fault if it scars them for life."

Rix scoffs. "They're made of tough stuff."

I have to agree with him, but I'm tense as I wait to hear what's coming next.

First, it's unintelligible yelling. Then, "You bitch! You killed him! I know you're behind that glass! I'm not going to rest until I ruin the career that you stole! Next time, I won't just put nails in your tire or take off your mirror, I'll take you out!"

My hand is on the Cadillac's door handle before he finishes yelling. I'm ready to rush the station and get Temperance out of there.

"That's definitely him. Please tell me you're going to nail his balls to the wall for threatening her," I hear Valentina say, confidence in her tone that slows my knee-jerk reaction.

"Damn fucking right. You're going to arrest him. Charge him with every fucking thing you can. That piece of shit is nuts, and he's not getting anywhere near my wife or her girl ever again. You hear me, Mac?"

That comes from Rix, and I release the door handle and take a deep breath.

"Ms. Ransom, can you confirm that Mr. Riddel put nails in your tire and damaged your mirror?"

"Yes. Absolutely. I didn't know it was him, but those incidents did happen. Roadside assistance took pictures of the tire. They're in my email. I can also get you pictures of the mirror."

"Good. Let's get your statements on each of those incidents, and you can send over the pictures when you get home. This asshole has a history of property damage, and now statements *in a police station* about escalating his behavior. I don't expect the judge is going to like that."

I don't breathe easy until Temperance is out of that building and back within my reach.

The next thing on my to-do list as soon as this mess Ransom got us all into is taken care of? Figure out how to get my life back so I never have to let her walk into a situation like this alone again.

I have no fucking clue how I'm going to do it, but I will.

I have no choice.

THIRTY-TWO
TEMPERANCE

"You look beautiful," Kane tells me as he stands in the living room and I step out of the bedroom in my brand-new *oh my God, I'm having my own art showing* dress.

"You think so? It isn't too much? Too little? Too underwhelming?"

He reaches out and grasps my hand. "Perfect. You look fucking perfect."

It's times like this when I wish I had a full-length mirror in my tiny apartment, but when I look at Kane, I realize I don't need one. I can see everything I need to know reflected in his icy blue eyes.

The only thing I don't see . . . is his suit.

"I thought you brought clothes to change into?" I ask.

He nods. "I did." He glances down at the jeans he's wearing. "You see them."

That's when it hits me.

"You're not going with me?" A stab of hurt pierces my chest.

"I don't want people asking questions about me when tonight is all about *you*."

Even though I'm devastated to hear his answer, something about it warms me. No one has ever had my best interest in mind as much as Kane does.

But this time, he's wrong.

"I need you with me, Kane. I *want* you with me. Tonight wouldn't be happening without you, and it won't be the same if you're not there."

He opens his mouth to respond, and I hold up a hand.

"I don't want to hear your arguments. I'm not taking no for an answer. You have an alias you use in public. You're using it tonight."

He snags my hand and lifts it to his mouth, pressing a kiss to my palm. "It's the most important night of your life—"

"Which is why you need to be there. I'm not walking into my first showing alone."

His features soften. "You sure you want me beside you? Even as Ken Sax?"

Sometimes, I swear the man is dense, but I'll lay it out for him in words he can't misunderstand.

"It doesn't matter what your name is. I always want you beside me. I love you."

"All right, princess. You got me."

When I walk into Noble Art, even with Kane beside me and no one in the gallery but Valentina, Trinity, a few other employees, and the serving staff, my stomach twists and flips.

What if everyone hates my work? It's one thing to watch it go for the highest bid when no one knows it's yours. And yet another thing completely when it's sold without me having to witness any of the negotiations or discussion.

This is a totally different ball game. In half an hour, this gallery will—God willing—be full of art patrons, and my job is to circulate among them and talk about my work in a way that makes me sound classy and confident.

I'm not sure I'm capable of that.

Kane's hand squeezes mine in a tight grip. "Hey. Look at me."

I turn to find his gaze on me.

"You can do this. You were born to do this, Temperance. I know it."

I shake my head because all my old insecurities are pushing to the forefront. "I feel like a fraud. Like someone is going to laugh and ask why they filled the room with scrap metal when there's supposed to be a sophisticated art showing taking place."

"That's not going to happen, so put it out of your mind."

He can't know that, though.

"What if no one buys anything, and Valentina is out all this time and effort and money?"

As if summoned by me saying her name, Valentina appears beside us. She presses a glass of champagne into my hand.

"Take this and drink it. You look like you need it."

"With the state of my stomach, I'm not sure champagne is the best idea right now."

Valentina gives me a sympathetic smile before she spins around to grab a bottle of water off the table behind her and trades me. "Trust me, I've been in your shoes. You're going to do great, even without liquid courage. Put your game face on. Go out there and act like the artist you are, and let people see your passion for your work. Tell them what you told me as we unloaded each one of them. The exhaust pipe that came off the Chevy Nova. The rearview mirror from the Land Rover. The sheet metal from a body panel of an old Willys jeep. How you saw those pieces and had a vision of giving them a second life instead of letting them get scrapped. You have a gift, Temperance. I wouldn't be doing this if I didn't believe that."

She throws my words and explanations from earlier this week back at me, and one by one, the knots in my stomach loosen.

"You really think people want to hear those stories?" I take a drink of water.

"Yes. Absolutely. That's what makes these pieces so

special. You take everyday objects and turn them into magic. Showings are incredible for patrons because it's the only time they truly get to experience an artist's passion as they explain their work. That's why I have no doubt we're both going to be pleasantly surprised tonight."

"But—"

"But nothing. I wouldn't have gotten so many RSVPs if no one wanted to buy a damn thing. I don't even know how we're going to fit everyone in this building. My fire inspector better not be working tonight, that's all I can say. Now, introduce me to your man. I don't think we've met."

Before I can say anything, Rix joins us.

"You better not be planning on bribing a public official, babe. It ain't a good idea."

Valentina laughs. "If I do, you're going to pretend you didn't hear a damn thing." Her gaze slides to Kane. "I'm Valentina Hendrix, and this is my gallery."

"Ken Sax." He shakes her hand, handling all this better than I do.

Valentina, Rix, Kane, and I make small talk until the first guest arrives and wants to speak to the artist.

Lord help me.

I'm the artist.

THIRTY-THREE
KANE

As the room fills, Temperance shines. I'm proud as hell as I watch her work the crowd, speaking to one art lover after another.

She hasn't yet noticed the two sold tags on the pieces I couldn't let be sold to attendees. I know she and I made a deal, but I'd rather beg her forgiveness for this transgression than ask her permission.

One is the couple in the throes of ecstasy that there was no way anyone else was taking home, and the other is the sugar skull she and I spent the afternoon finding the perfect piece to finish it. Do I care that I dropped six figures here tonight? Hell no. It was the best money I've spent since the auction where I got the fleur de lis without knowing it was hers.

Over the next hour, I watch as Valentina discreetly places sold tags on four other sculptures.

I hope, finally, Temperance understands that her

work is valued by everyone in this room tonight, and not just me.

Valentina Hendrix's cop husband watches me closely as the night wears on, but I don't show any sign of concern. Mostly because I'm not concerned. There's no way he can connect me to anything I've ever done. I'm a ghost when it comes to my job. The only place I step into the light is when Temperance is involved, and my alias is rock solid.

In fact, everything is going perfectly tonight . . . until I spot a familiar face in the crowd.

Fuck. What the hell is he doing here?

Giles weaves his way through the sculptures, but is blocked from Temperance by a small group of guests.

I move in his direction and feel the cop's stare boring holes into my back. There's a good possibility he could recognize Giles too. Years in the state government have kept his picture in the media.

"Damn, we even got politicians here tonight." Rix's voice comes from beside me, catching me off guard. Fucker moves fast. "Your girl should be proud of the crowd she's drawn."

"Whether she is or not, I'm proud enough for ten people."

He laughs. "I know the feeling. Valentina didn't think her stuff was good enough for her own damn gallery. It ate at me. Killed me that she couldn't see how incredible her talent was. I hated that for her. Had to change her mind the hard way."

"How'd you do that?"

"Put one of them up on the wall without her knowing, and wouldn't you know, it sold the next day."

"That's one way to go about it."

"It was what she needed. I saw it. She didn't. So I took care of it."

I'm reading between the lines to figure out if the cop is trying to deliver a silent message, and I don't have to guess for long.

"I don't like you, Sax. Don't trust you. I think you're hiding something, and Valentina has taken Temperance under her wing, which means she's got a tether to you. I need to know what the fuck I'm dealing with by my wife bringing your woman into her world, and you're gonna tell me."

I keep my features schooled and show no reaction. "I don't know what you're worried about, but I'm guessing it's those overactive cop instincts sending you false alarms."

The cop shoots me a sharp look. "I recognize someone who's seen way too much. I see that look in the mirror every fucking day, so it's not something I can miss."

I turn to face him, taking my attention off Giles. "What are you after, man?"

"Assurances that if you've got shit swirling around you, it won't touch my woman or this gallery ever again." He glances at the new glass window. "I don't take kindly to shit blowing back on my family, and there's nothing I won't do to protect them."

I lift my chin, actually respecting him even more for laying it out like that. "I appreciate the sentiment. More than you know. But that window didn't have shit to do with me, and it wasn't blowback."

"Then why the fuck didn't you show at the station when she came in? You don't strike me as the type to let your woman walk into something like that alone."

When did cops get so fucking perceptive?

"I had other business."

"Or you didn't want to be seen in a cop shop."

"Look, man, whatever you're looking for, you won't find it. I'm here for Temperance, and that's it."

Rix appraises me. "Maybe. But why are you so fucking interested in Giles?"

THIRTY-FOUR
TEMPERANCE

"Finally, a chance to speak to the beautiful artist herself. What an incredible opportunity."

The voice, a semi-familiar one, sends the hairs on my arms rising. I turn to see Giles smiling at me, and I want to shoot the smug grin off his face. If this man is a human trafficker, he deserves much worse.

Then I remember—*he's seen me without a mask at the club.* Maybe he won't recognize me. It's the only thing I can possibly hope. It might be dumb, but what other choice do I have?

I hold out a hand. "I'm Temperance Ransom." I try to add another pleasantry, like it's a pleasure to meet him, but I can't make my lips form the words. Instead, I go quiet.

He takes my hand, and immediately I want to bathe in sanitizer.

"Ransom, you say? That's a unique last name."

Fuck. Fuck. Fuck.

He knows my brother. How could I forget? Because Magnolia hooked him up with Giles in the trafficking.

I swallow the lump in my throat and pretend I don't know shit about anything. It's the only way I'm going to make it through this without doing something stupid.

"Are you interested in a piece? Can I tell you more about my art?" I redirect the conversation to safer territory.

"I'd like to hear more about you, my dear. After all, artists are truly my favorite kind of people."

There's a double meaning to everything that comes out of this man's mouth. I know it.

"I'm not that interesting. Just a girl who's good with a hammer, saw, and welder." I inject a bit of warning in my tone.

"Fascinating. And where did you pick up these talents? Working at Seven Sinners?"

My hackles rise. He's been looking into me. But why?

"Excuse me?"

"That's where you used to be employed, is it not? The distillery here in town. The one where there was a silent auction, and a friend of mine was outbid on one of your pieces. Although, at that time, I believe it was under someone else's name. Who was that again?"

I don't like this man and have no idea what he's digging at, but it can't be good.

Kane is beside me before I can scan the crowd to find him. *Sweet Lord, please don't let Giles recognize him.*

"Senator Giles, it's a pleasure to meet you, sir. Glad to see politicians can be art fans as well."

"Of course. Actually . . ." Giles pauses, and my plea goes unanswered. "I've seen you before, haven't I? What was your name again?"

Kane holds out a hand. "I don't believe we've ever had the pleasure of being introduced." I have no idea how Kane acts so well, but he's a master. "I'm Ken Sax."

"Interesting." Giles's gaze travels from Kane to me and back again. "Such a striking couple. If you're ever interested in a little more *fun*, I believe you do know where to find me."

I choke on the water I'm sipping to keep myself from speaking, but Kane doesn't react.

"Now, what can you tell me about this piece?" Giles points to the large sculpture of the couple I made similar to Harriet's, and immediately I wish I hadn't. "I absolutely love the carnal nature of it. Reminds me of you two. I have a wonderful place to display it where it could be admired and appreciated."

He's talking about the club. I know it.

Kane comes to the rescue again. "I believe that one is sold, sir. Someone else clearly had the same good taste you do." There's a hard edge to his voice, but I'm more shocked by his words.

"Sold? I sold a piece?" I look at the tag tucked by the base, and sure enough, it says SOLD right on it.

"Over half of them are already taken, actually."

My mouth drops open as I stare up at him. "Are you serious?"

"Absolutely."

"I suppose that means I need to go look at what's still available if I want a chance to snap one up," Giles says before slinking away, giving us both one last glance.

But not even Giles can detract from the euphoria of that moment.

I sold art! At a showing! I'm not a failure.

That damn burn behind my eyes is back again, but I refuse to shed a single tear tonight. Even a happy one.

"I did it," I whisper.

"Congratulations, princess."

As Kane slides his arm around me, a thought strikes.

"Please tell me you didn't buy them all."

He shakes his head. "Only two. The other four went to people I've never met. But you better be damned sure I'll be adding their names to my list in case they ever go to sell. I get first dibs."

A happy sigh works its way free of my chest. "You know, you do live with the artist. She'll make you whatever you want, whenever."

He looks down at me, and even I can't miss the pride in his eyes. "I know. But it's a hell of a lot more fun to plot how I'm going to get them from the other people who wanted them just as badly as I do."

"What about—"

Kane shakes his head, cutting me off. "You're not allowed to worry about him tonight. Tonight is about *you*. Enjoy it. He won't bother you again."

Kane's right. I'm not going to let Giles taint this experience for me. *Tonight is mine.*

THIRTY-FIVE

KANE

I t takes everything I have to let Temperance step away from my side, knowing that Giles is in the room. For the next hour, I keep my attention split between them, and Rix watches me as he sips on a drink.

He might as well be wearing a sign that says *I'm not going to let you out of my sight until I figure out what the fuck you're doing.*

He can watch all he wants, but he's not going to get a damn bit of information from me. At least, not yet. If Giles and some of his other politician friends are scum-of-the-earth human traffickers, maybe a better punishment than one of my bullets is turning them over to the cops to let the system expose their crimes and render judgment.

Even though unlikely, it's something to think about.

Thankfully, Giles doesn't make a purchase, and the

rest of the night passes with nothing but smiles from Temperance, because he stays the fuck away from her.

I'm not doing anything to fuck up tonight for her, and neither is anyone else.

Putting those thoughts aside, I turn as the door chime jingles and Temperance's former boss, Keira Mount, and Yve Titan walk in the door together, without their infamous husbands.

There go the rest of the sculptures, I think with a smile.

THIRTY-SIX
TEMPERANCE

"So you'll still come to Frisky Whiskey Night at the Pretty Kitty?" Yve asks, and I look at Keira.

"Do you mind?"

My boss's head jerks back. "Please tell me you didn't really ask that question. You're welcome everywhere, Temperance. I'd take you back in a heartbeat if you ever changed your mind."

Since I officially quit, I haven't been sure how to act around Keira, but apparently, I'm the only one with the hang-up.

"Then that's a yes," Yve says. "Now you can't back out. My work here is done. I got a sculpture, finally got to see you looking incredible and light years different than you did the last time I saw you, and—"

"What do you mean?" I ask, trying to think of the last time I saw Yve.

"We came to your apartment. Harriet let us in. We brought food, and flowers, and cards, but you were asleep in a corner, curled up in a chair. Don't you remember?"

My mind races to remember what she's talking about, and I come up blank.

I shake my head.

"Me, Valentina, Ariel . . ." She trails off when she sees no recognition on my face.

"I'm really sorry. I was in a dark place. Everything from that month is basically a blur. If Harriet hadn't forced food into me, I probably would've starved."

Yve's expression softens with a hint of pity, but I don't need it now, not that I can tell her that I don't need it. "I'm so sorry anyway. It's hard to be alone in the world. Losing family is never easy."

"Thank you," I say quietly, accepting her hug. Even though it makes me feel like a fraud, it's comforting. I didn't realize I had support from such amazing friends.

On the flip side, it's also a reminder that Rafe has to stay dead. He can never come back to life in Louisiana. The realization hits me hard, and a shaft of unexpected pain stabs me in the gut.

It's okay, though. At least he's alive.

"Now, can you tell me about this piece? I didn't see it before, but my husband would die for it. And since he's on a business trip, it's my duty to surprise him." Yve points to a large crown mounted on the wall.

By the time Yve makes her second purchase, there are only two pieces left for sale, and my imposter syndrome starts to fade.

I can do this.

I can have my dream.

THIRTY-SEVEN
KANE

L ater that night, after Temperance's first sold-out showing, she rests her head on my chest.

"I can't believe this is real. That this is my life."

She looks up at me with wonder shining in her eyes, and I vow to do everything I can to keep that look on her face for as long as I live.

"Believe it. I'm so damn proud of you, princess. You deserve every single bit of it."

She traces one of my tattoos with her finger. "You know, I made a bucket list when I decided I wasn't going to give up on life. Actually, Harriet mostly made me."

"Oh yeah?" I meet her dark gaze. "What was on it?"

"A few things I can already check off, actually."

"Like what?"

"Introduce myself as an artist, and *be happy*."

A feeling of contentment, unlike anything I've ever

known, builds in me. "I'm glad I can make you happy. What else do we still need to check off?"

"You want to do it with me?"

"Do you really need to ask that?"

She smiles. "Drink wine at Harriet's vineyard in Italy, and travel the world."

"Is that all?"

"I can cross the last one off, and thankfully not because I completed it."

"What's that?"

"Honor my brother's memory." A feeling of fore-boding pervades my contentment when she says it and then looks back up at me. "Because he's going to be safe, right?"

I nod because there's no other choice. I just hope I'm not lying.

THIRTY-EIGHT
TEMPERANCE

"You came!" Yve says as I walk through the door of Pretty Kitty a week after my showing at Noble Art—which Valentina called a smash hit. On top of buying the crown sculpture, Yve commissioned another piece, and I've been working on it for three days.

"I snuck away from working on a certain custom piece, so I hope the customer isn't upset that it's going to be a few more days in production."

She smiles. "As long as you leave here with lingerie and a smile, I've got no complaints," she says, crossing the room and wrapping an arm around me to squeeze.

Six months ago, I didn't know what it was like to have women friends, but it seems I've been adopted by several, and hugs are now a commonplace thing. It's crazy how life can change.

Before Kane came into my life, I was working at the

distillery, assuming that's what I was going to do with the rest of my life, and hadn't had sex in forever. Now I'm in a lingerie store, surrounded by familiar faces, and I'm going to pick out some killer stuff so I can shock the hell out of my man and be a *very* bad girl.

In fact, I feel the urge to role-play coming back. We may not be able to go back to the club anymore because Kane doesn't think it's safe, but my need for what he gave me there hasn't disappeared. I'll just reclaim it at home.

A plan is already taking shape in my mind when I see Ariel holding up a sinful black bra-and-panty set.

Her eyes brighten when she sees me. "Hey, girl! You look fabulous. How are you doing? Are you okay? Can I do anything? Do you need anyone added to the no-fly list?"

Her over-the-top greeting reminds me just how much I like the girl genius who is more computer hacker than CEO.

"I'm good. Things are going well. Life is finding a new rhythm, and I'm hanging in there." It's hard not to tell her the truth, but keeping Rafe's secret is at the top of the priority list, so I have no choice.

"Good. We were so worried about you. I even did a few things I shouldn't have . . ."

Oh Jesus. "Like?"

She stares at the ceiling for a moment.

"Ariel?"

With a wince, she meets my gaze. "I hacked a few satellites and found out where it all went down. I know about the cover-up." She keeps her voice low so no one can overhear her.

"Please tell me you haven't told anyone."

She glances over to where Keira stands near Yve, making sure the whiskey is being enjoyed.

"No. Everything I could figure led right back to a place I don't want to mess with because I don't have a death wish."

I know she's talking about Mount, and for the first time, I'm really glad he's a super-scary mofo who is married to my former boss.

"You should definitely not dig any further into that situation," I tell her, matching her tone of voice.

Ariel nods. "I got that. But . . . I'm still not going to feel okay about leaving it be until you get justice for what happened."

"Oh Lord, what business are you sticking your nose into now?" The question comes from the gorgeous blonde stepping closer to us that I remember as Vanessa from the girls' night I went to at Valentina's.

"Not important," I reply, just as Ariel says, "Nothing."

"I'm around sneaky teenagers all day, and I know you're both full of shit," Vanessa says.

"Trust me when I say you don't want to know," I tell her.

Vanessa tilts her head. "Please tell me Ariel isn't

hacking into something that's going to get you both killed."

"I don't do that stuff anymore."

"Right. Like I believe that for a second." She glances behind Ariel. "Where's the laptop?"

"Yve forbid me from bringing it. Again."

Vanessa shakes her head and laughs. "I can't believe you actually left home without the thing."

Ariel's fingers twitch. "I usually don't. You never know when you'll need to hack into North Korea's missile guidance system to save the free world."

I let out an uncomfortable laugh, not sure if she's joking or not.

"I'm off to buy something that's going to blow Con's mind. You two . . ." Vanessa looks at both Ariel and me like we're as guilty as the teenagers she spends time around. "Stay out of trouble."

As soon as she turns her back, Ariel shoots me a sideways glance. "If there's information you need that you don't want to talk about here, come to my place tomorrow."

I give her a nod because I don't want to get myself into any trouble. But . . . there's definitely information I need. We need the connection between Giles and the human traffickers. We need to find Lagarto. And I want my brother home safe and sound.

"I don't care what you're talking about, but tonight is about lingerie," Yve says, joining our group. "So go find some, drink the amazing whiskey, and spend all your money."

"Girl, you don't stock enough lingerie for us to spend all our money. Didn't you know we're ballers?" Ariel says with a smile.

Hearing her talk so easily and confidently about who and what she is gives me a new goal.

Someday I'm going to be a badass like Ariel.

The door chimes again, and I see another familiar face.

"You made it!" Yve calls, and the dark-haired gallery owner joins us.

"Pass up whiskey and driving my husband wild with something naughty? Wouldn't miss it for the world." Valentina sees me next. "Temperance! I'm so glad you're here. I was going to call you in the morning because I need your wire-transfer information."

Wire-transfer information. It makes me sound so fancy, which is definitely not the case.

"Whatever you need," I say. "Although I have no idea what that information is."

"I can get it for her," Ariel says with a smile. "But you probably don't want me to."

"Oh Lord. Don't get the girl started hacking into all our bank accounts. She'll probably put more money *in* them because she's a weird-ass benevolent hacker. Or start college funds for all our kids." This comment comes from Yve.

Ariel flips her the bird with a smile as she sips a glass of water.

"Why are you drinking water and not whiskey?" Valentina asks, her eyes narrowed.

"Why do you think?" Ariel replies with a hint of attitude.

"Oh my God! Really? You're—"

"Knocked up and can't stop crying when I'm happy or feeling like I'm going to puke pretty much all the time."

"Holy shit!" A woman with deep auburn hair walks in the door, and she gives a little shimmy. "The girl genius is knocked up! I didn't expect to hear *that* tonight!"

"Elle! You came." Vanessa squeals and hugs the woman.

As everyone catches up with the new arrival, my mind is stuck on what Ariel said. Crying all the time and constantly feeling like you want to puke . . .

No. Way.

Seriously. There's no way I'm . . . I do the math in my head.

Not possible. Is it?

Maybe.

There's a definite maybe.

I should be freaking the fuck out about the possibility of being pregnant, especially right now, but instead, a tiny kernel of hope blooms inside me.

The timing wouldn't be great, and I'm not going to jump to conclusions, but . . . *wow*.

I bite down on my lip as my mouth curves into a smile. How crazy would that be? One thing is for sure, though.

I'm not saying anything until I know one way or the other.

THIRTY-NINE
KANE

W hen Temperance walks out of the lingerie store, I'm glad to see she has a bag in her hand and a smile on her face. She needed tonight. Something good and normal.

Through the brightly lit windows, I watch her give good-bye hugs to her newfound friends, so glad she has that. I want her to have that. I want her to have everything.

I get out of the car and open the door for her. "My lady," I say, gesturing for her to enter.

"Gallant. You're totally hoping I bought something scandalous, and now you want to see it on, don't you?" she asks as she slides into the seat.

"That's not why I'm opening your door for you, but I wouldn't say no regardless."

"Good," she says with a smile. "Because it's *definitely* scandalous."

I close her door and round the hood to get in the driver's side. "Where to tonight?"

We've been splitting our time between Temperance's apartment and the warehouse, depending on what hours she's working, but we've spent the majority of nights at her place. Thankfully, Harriet has been out of town quite a bit, otherwise I'd be worried the noises we make upstairs would give the old woman a heart attack.

Then again, it's Harriet . . .

I'm not complaining, though. I don't care where we are as long as I fall asleep beside her.

"Let's go to the warehouse . . ."

When Temperance trails off, I immediately wonder what she has planned.

Since we stopped going to the club because of Giles, I've wondered whether she was getting everything she needed from me, or if she still needs that dark edge of the voyeurism that brought us together.

When I pull into the garage, she's out of the car before I can open her door.

"Eager?"

She nods. "Give me twenty minutes before you come up, though. I promise it'll be worth the wait."

"I'd wait forever for you."

Her face softens, and I lean in for a kiss before she heads upstairs to no doubt blow my mind with whatever she has planned.

FORTY
TEMPERANCE

W hen Kane walks upstairs after waiting like I asked, I hear him check the bedroom first. But he won't find me there. No, I'm down the hall in an office that I don't think he's ever used based on the completely clear state of the desk.

Which works perfectly for my purposes.

Regardless of how our lives are going to change in the near future, whether from the suspicions I now have or because of the mess my brother dragged us into, I need one night to not worry about any of it.

I need one night of just *us* and what originally brought us together.

Kane's not slow, so it doesn't take him long to find me in the office, leaning against the edge of the desk in my brand-new purchase—which shows more than it conceals.

I don't need to hide anything from him. I just want to continue to tempt him.

"I didn't realize we had a meeting planned for this evening," Kane says, his icy gaze sweeping over me with approval.

"Your seat, *sir*." I nod to the armchair in the corner that has the only dim light in the room above it.

Kane sits, his legs spread and his hands resting on his knees, and he watches me where I stand in black stilettos.

The things I want to do to that man . . . or let him do to me.

"What's on the agenda for tonight's meeting?"

"Just a little temptation."

"I think you've miscalculated."

I tilt my head, swinging my hair to the side. "How's that?"

"You're no little temptation. You're the ultimate." His gaze starts at my feet and caresses my body as it rises. "Those black stilettos. Sexy as fuck. Those stockings? I want to peel them down with my teeth before I push those tiny red-and-gold panties aside and taste the sweet pussy you're hiding."

In the beginning, it was watching someone else that unleashed the fire within me. But now, I realize that was just the catalyst to make me go after the real prize—a man who could give me everything I needed, in bed and out. Who could help me shed my inhibitions. Forget everything except how he makes me feel.

"I want that. I want everything from you. Everything you've promised me."

His gaze reaches my face. "I sure as hell hope so, because it's already yours."

He's speaking in generalities, and I'm thinking in specifics, but he'll understand soon enough. *Like in ten seconds.* My core pulses at the thought of what's coming.

"Do you want to see the rest?" I ask, a hint of tease in my voice.

"Always."

I push off the desk and slowly turn in a circle, and I know the moment he sees the lack of material in a very specific place in my lingerie choice.

"Sweet fucking Christ. Princess . . ."

I glance over my shoulder to see him gripping the arms of the chair. "You like?"

His nostrils flare as he loosens his grip and stands. "No. I fucking love you. Every inch of you." He crosses the floor separating us and stops close behind me. His breath touches my shoulder as his hand covers one cheek of my ass and gives it a delicious squeeze.

I release a soft moan.

"You flash this beautiful ass at me, and there's no way in hell I can stop from touching it."

"I want you to touch it." I meet his stare. "I want even more than that."

I didn't know his blue eyes could burn so hot before this moment. Kane's palm slides from my cheek to trail two fingers up my crack.

"You want me to fuck this sweet ass?"

"Yes."

He groans, his eyelids dropping before he moves, and jerks me back against his chest so he can take my mouth. As his lips devour mine, I give myself over to his kiss.

When we're both breathless, he pulls back and stares into my eyes.

"You. Are. Mine."

"I know."

His lips skim down my neck to where it meets my shoulder, and the arousal he's stoked burns even hotter.

Since the moment I picked this particular pair of panties off the rack, I knew what I wanted tonight. That's why there's a plug and a bottle of lube already here.

"I bought supplies too . . . in the drawer." My voice is breathy, and we've barely gotten started.

Kane pulls back. "I already knew you were perfect, but this seals it."

I start to bend over, but he stops me.

"Not yet, princess. First, I'm going to enjoy these pretty tits and eat that tight little pussy."

I don't know what it is about when his mouth turns filthy, but it kicks everything up to the next level.

He turns me around and both hands wrap around my waist to lift me onto the desk. His lips find my nipples through the sheer lace of the bra, and he sucks them into his mouth one at a time.

When my head is thrown back, he finally reaches for the clasp and it releases. Inch by inch, he pulls the bra down my arms, and my skin tingles in the wake of where his fingers touch. He plays with my nipples until they're as hard as diamonds and I'm begging.

"You need more?"

"Yes. I want to come."

"Then that's exactly what you're going to do."

Kane drops to his knees in front of me and spreads my legs wide. "Heels on the desk. Lean back."

If not for the tiny patch of lace covering me, I'd be completely exposed. And then Kane tugs that to the side and I am.

"So fucking pretty." He leans forward to swipe with his tongue. "And so fucking delicious."

"Please—"

"Oh, I will please you, princess. I swear it."

His hands wrap around my inner thighs, holding me open, and then he moves in.

Tongue. Teeth. Lips. He uses everything at his disposal to make me scream his name and beg for him to push me over the edge. But every time I get close, he pulls back.

"Kane!"

"You dying to come?"

"Yes!"

"Then you're *almost* ready."

When I set tonight's events in motion, I didn't realize

I was signing myself up for the most sensual torture imaginable, but apparently, I miscalculated.

Kane rises, and I want to shove his face back between my legs, but his blue gaze is intent on me.

"Where are the supplies?"

I jerk my head back. "Top drawer. Right side."

"Fucking amazing woman." He finds them and wastes no time setting the lube and plug beside me.

"Hurry."

But instead of flipping me over and giving me what I'm begging for, he strokes two fingers down my cheek.

"I'm glad you asked for what you need, Temperance. I will always make sure you have it. Always."

"And what about what you need?" I ask.

"You give it to me just by breathing."

A wave of emotion washes over me, and I wrap a hand around his neck and crush my mouth to his. When I finally pull back, I tell him, "I love you, Kane."

He bows his head, touching his forehead to mine. "Come what may, I will *always* love you."

When he pulls back, he offers me a hand and I take it. Gently, he spins me around to face the desk and I bend over, reveling in the press of the cold wood against my nipples.

He caresses my ass, cupping a cheek. "Have you missed me playing with this sweet ass of yours?"

I swallow. "Yes."

"I won't neglect it again. I promise."

He releases his grip on my cheek as he slides a finger

under the outer strap of my panties and follows it down toward my center.

"So fucking wet."

He's *so close* to where I want his touch. He dips a finger into my wetness and circles my entrance.

"You want my cock here?" he asks.

"*Yes.*" My voice breaks on my plea, but he doesn't comply. Kane drags his finger back to circle my rear entrance.

"What about here?"

God help me, but I feel like I've never wanted something more.

"Please, Kane. I need—"

"You're gonna get everything you need. Don't doubt that. But first, I need something from you."

"What? Anything."

"I want to hear you tell me you love me again."

"I love you." I whisper it, and then I yell. "I love you, Kane Savage! Until my last breath, I love you!"

He presses a kiss to my shoulder. "And I'll love you through this life and the next."

"Yes. Through this life and the next."

That's the moment he plunges a finger inside me at the same time he finds my clit, and my orgasm crashes over me. I arch on the desk, trying for more pressure, more contact, more everything.

Kane tugs my crotchless panties down over my ass, and I shimmy to shake them free before letting them drop to the floor. I'm primed and ready.

Anticipation heightens every sensation because I know what's coming. When the drizzle of lube hits my ass, I tremble with excitement. I'm ready. I want this.

I need this.

"First, we'll stretch you out." He presses a well-lubed finger against my ass, and it breaches more smoothly than it did last time.

"Oh God." My nerve endings tingle and feel like they're practically cheering.

"So fucking tight. You're going to strangle my cock, and I'm going to love every single second of it."

He fucks my ass with his finger slowly, teasing me with every movement while my vision turns hazy, and I realize it's because my eyes are closing. I let them slide shut and give myself over to the sensations.

Kane slides a second finger inside, and the burn increases deliciously. "Can you take me?"

"Yes." No hesitation. No question.

"Temptress."

He separates his fingers in a scissor-like motion, testing the muscle, and I squirm on the desk. When he pulls free, it's to push a plug into my ass and notch his cock against my pussy.

"Fuck, you're so wet."

I love the desperation in his tone, just like I loved the struggle in his eyes while I sucked him off. I love knowing that I can do this to him. That he wants me as badly as I want him.

He pushes inside, and I'm beyond full. My ass flexes against the plug as Kane pounds inside me.

My cries spur him on and my orgasm builds. He reaches beneath me and finds my clit, and I shatter.

"Kane!" I scream his name as the pleasure takes me under and his thrusts keep coming, harder and faster until he pulls free.

"It's time."

"Please."

He pulls the plug from my ass and tosses it aside before more lube coats my back entrance.

"Tell me if you can't take it. I'm going to go slow."

The head presses against the tight ring of muscle, and I relax into the sensation. It slips inside, and for a moment, I feel like I'm being split wide open.

"Holy shit. I don't know if it's going to fit. You might be too big."

His fingers find my clit and once again set another orgasm building inside me. Against all odds, I press back against him, seeking more as he teases me into loving this new sensation.

"Good girl. Take it slow."

An inch at a time, I take his cock. My nerve endings scream in a dizzying new kind of pleasure. It's a dark, twisted sensation that plays on everything I never wanted to admit about myself.

"Your turn," I whisper, taking a chance.

"You sure?"

"Yes. Just go slow."

The line between pleasure and pain blurs as Kane takes over, keeping my clit buzzing at the same time he fills my ass and retreats, over and over.

My pussy soaks the desk, and my throat grows hoarse from screaming his name.

When I finally come, every inch of my skin seems to shimmer with the sensation. I feel like I'm floating off the desk, and then Kane roars as he pumps his climax into my ass.

After he cleans me up, he carries me to bed, and I know for certain that this is exactly what I needed.

FORTY-ONE
TEMPERANCE

S unday afternoon, after I hit a good stopping point on my commissioned piece for Yve, I get a text.

ARIEL: You coming over? My skills are at your disposal.

Kane's not going to like me having my hacker friend dig into Giles, but he's not here for me to tell. He left a half hour ago in a Land Rover to "run a few errands," which I assume means he's out doing something more than just getting groceries. But I trust him, and I didn't ask questions. Instead, I kissed him good-bye and told him I loved him.

Now I wish I'd asked more questions, so at least I would know how long he's going to be gone.

I shoot Ariel a text saying I'll be on my way in a half hour, and one to Kane telling him I'm going to Ariel's for some girl time.

She responds with an address and a string of emojis, but Kane doesn't respond at all.

You better be safe, I think, *or I'll kill you myself.*

I take a quick shower and throw my hair up into a messy bun before pulling on cutoffs and a black tank top. To be safe, I take the Audi I know has bullet-resistant glass and armored doors. *It'll make Kane feel better about me not being here when he gets back,* I tell myself.

When I pull up to the gate in front of the address Ariel sent me, I realize I truly had no idea what I was getting into with her. It's not a house back there, it's a mansion.

I give my name to the person on the other end of the speaker box, and the gate swings open.

I park at the end of the long driveway, on a cement pad off to the side, so as not to block the massive garage or the entrance to the house.

Ariel yanks the door open before I'm out of my car. "You made it!"

I make my way up to the entrance, trying to reconcile the monstrous house with the messy bun and HANGRY HANGRY HIPPO T-shirt Ariel is wearing.

"You seriously are a baller, aren't you?"

She smirks. "I'm a CEO, and my companies make cool shit. Ergo, I make a pile of cash. The house was a rental, but I fell in love with it. Wouldn't you know that the mysterious Mr. Mount decided he was cool selling it to me?"

"Wait—" I glance at the beautiful entryway, modern

and sleek, with a different eye. "This was Mount's house?"

She nods. "Apparently one of them he didn't use anymore. And even though I've dismantled his security system and installed my own, I still wonder if he can see everything that happens in here. That dude is freaking scary."

She has no concept of just how scary he is. All I do is nod in agreement.

"And yet, your former boss *married* him and lived to tell about it."

I think of the way Keira smiles and practically makes heart-eyes when she talks about him. "She didn't just live to tell about it . . . she's truly happy."

"Bitch be crazy, that's all I can say. Anyway, that's not why you're here. You're here for me to work my magic." Ariel leads me through a modern kitchen with gleaming stainless appliances to a long table that faces an incredible view of Lake Pontchartrain.

"Nice digs."

"Mount had good taste. I didn't change much," Ariel says as she pulls out a chair in front of her laptop. She stretches her hands and fingers before sitting down and looking up at me. "Now, what information are we digging for this time?"

"How do you know I need more information?"

She tilts her head as I sit next to her. "Because knowledge is power. Why wouldn't you want more? So . . . tell me and we can get to it. I won't even charge you.

But I do take payment in cookies if you know how to bake."

I laugh. "I'll buy you some cookies."

"Fair enough. Now, go. I'm ready."

I swallow, not sure how much I should say to her. "This is not a good situation. *At all.* Like . . . no one can know what we talk about or what you find."

"Shit. That kind of stuff?"

I nod and Ariel stands, shutting her laptop.

I blink at her. "What are you—"

"We're moving this to where I handle the super-secure shit. I live for this stuff. You have no idea. Come on."

I follow Ariel through a massive master suite into a closet and look away as she punches in a code. A panel opens, and she waves a hand toward it.

"Welcome to my safe room."

I step inside what looks like a luxurious dressing room with ornate cabinets lining two walls, and an island in the center. Two large leather sofas are situated into a conversation area.

At least until Ariel comes in, closes the door, and hits some kind of button.

The whole room changes. The cabinets disappear to reveal a high-tech security center that looks a lot like what Kane has on the second floor of the warehouse.

"You have a bat cave."

Ariel grins at me. "I sure as hell do." She pulls up

chairs, and we settle in while she hooks up her laptop to what I assume is a secure hardline.

"You can cover your tracks?"

"Better than anyone else out there. I hacked the Pentagon seven times last year, and they never caught me. I'm the best."

Then she's exactly who I need. "Good, because these people are bad."

One of Ariel's red eyebrows goes up. "How bad?"

"*Bad*. The kind of people who don't deserve to actually be alive because they sell other people."

Ariel whips her head around to meet my gaze. "Whoa. Okay. So real super baddies. *Shit*. I got you. Now, give me a name or something and we'll start digging." She places her fingers on the keyboard and waits.

I'm almost afraid to say it out loud, because I definitely didn't get permission from Kane to do this first.

"Can you keep a secret?"

Ariel's expression turns solemn. "I'm keeping more secrets than I wish I was. I'm a vault. That's how hackers stay alive."

I suck in a breath. "Giles."

"First name?" Ariel asks.

"Lewis. He's a state senator and used to be a DA."

Her eyes widen as she shifts in the desk chair and flexes her fingers. "The plot thickens . . . Let's dig this motherfucker's entire past up and nail him for whatever he's doing."

FORTY-TWO
TEMPERANCE

Ariel isn't all talk. No, she's downright terrifying with how fast she digs into Giles's life.

"Widower. One son. Three homes. He pays his taxes, although he probably should be audited because his deductions are exceptionally high for his income. His credit card number has been stolen six times this year, which is impressive. Probably karma. He's got a prescription for Viagra from his doctor. He buys some kind of stamina supplement from China on a regular basis too." She talks as her fingers fly, unearthing everything she can on Giles, and I wait for her to hit pay dirt.

"What about criminal activity?"

"Nothing yet. I'm still digging, and there's no way he's good enough to cover his tracks when I'm on the hunt."

She continues spouting off random facts about

Giles's life, but nothing that relates to anything I'm looking to find. At least, not yet.

"He had a really high conviction rate as a DA. Like freakishly high for the number of cases that were prosecuted." Ariel pauses. "Ah . . . because his brother was the judge. Like that's not a major conflict of interest. Jesus. Who allowed that to happen?"

"Crooked parish, apparently."

"Whoa, the judge brother was murdered. Unsolved. Police suspected it was a hit related to a man he sent to prison whose exonerating evidence was 'lost' during the trial by the chief of police, who also died shortly after." She lowers her voice. "The guy on trial was someone related to the Mount organization." Ariel looks over at me. "But you knew all that already, didn't you?"

I say nothing but my mind is whirring.

"Interesting . . ." She turns back to the screen. "Strangely enough, the judge's stepson died six weeks earlier. Body was only identified by the dog tags they found on it. Nothing else was salvageable. He was an army sniper."

Her fingers stop moving.

"No one thought that was remotely coincidental? I mean, I know I'm into conspiracy theories, but it sounds to me like—"

"That's enough."

Ariel lifts her hands off the keyboard. "Because you're afraid of Mount . . . or is there another reason?"

"I can't tell you."

Her gaze narrows on me. She looks like she has a million and one questions she wants to ask, but she holds them in.

"Fair enough. Normally I'd be gung ho for digging into this, but when the name Mount comes up, I check myself. So . . . is this all you wanted, or is there another direction we can go to find out what you need to know?"

"Is there anything out there about a company Giles just bought a piece of?"

Ariel looks back to her computer. "He has a network of shell companies. It's damn near untraceable . . . but I'm better than he is. There's a bank account for one of them in the Caymans. It's active." She pauses. "Whoa."

"What?"

"Do you know who Magnolia Maison is?"

Goose bumps rise on my skin. "Yes."

"That company of his has been paying her on the regular." Ariel leans back in her chair. "Is there a reason a guy you suspect of human trafficking would be paying a madam protected by Mount?"

"Fuck. Kane thought she was lying."

Ariel's gaze cuts to mine. "Kane, huh?"

Fuck. It's the second time I've done it. First with Magnolia and now with Ariel.

"Please pretend you didn't hear that."

She crosses her arms. "I'm a hell of a lot more effective when I understand the big picture."

"I can't tell you."

She studies me. "You don't need to. I can read

218

between the lines. But what does Magnolia have to do with it?"

I swallow. "I don't know. But I need to know."

"Isn't she besties with Mount's wife?"

"Yeah."

"So . . . maybe we don't touch her."

"But if she's human trafficking . . ."

Ariel releases a sigh. "You're right. There's a chance he might not kill us."

"Wait, there's one other name, or sort of a name we can look into."

"I'm listening."

"Lagarto. It means—"

"Lizard in Portuguese. Of course a human trafficker would have a slimy nickname."

Then her fingers are off and moving again, and she's digging in the dark web for the man Rafe and Kane are hunting.

Ariel is quiet for nearly twenty minutes. For a girl that I'm pretty sure wasn't joking about disabling North Korean nukes, that seems like an awfully long time to have her digging for a piece of information.

"Anything?"

She shakes her head. "This guy's a motherfucking ghost. Chameleon would've been a better choice than Lizard. His name comes up plenty of places where other people are talking about him, but I need a real name before I can find him."

"Fuck."

"Right . . . wait . . ." Then Ariel pauses, turning the screen toward me. There's a black-and-white photo on the screen of a man wearing a big floppy hat.

"What?"

"Have you ever met a man who would wear a hat like that?"

"It's stupid-looking but not unbelievable."

"I know this is going to sound crazy, but what if . . . what if the Lizard isn't a *he*?"

"You think he could be . . ."

Ariel and I lock eyes.

No fucking way. That would explain way too much. Why Kane and Rafe haven't been able to track down the guy . . . because he's not a guy.

Her expression turns grim. "I've had crazier theories."

"Where is Magnolia right now?" I ask.

"Do you really want to go down this road?"

I think about my brother and Kane, and the lives we won't ever get to live fully until this is over.

"I don't have any other choice."

FORTY-THREE
KANE

"What the fuck? Are you serious?" I stare at Mount like he's just told me he has four balls and a double dick.

"Do you think I make up shit about human trafficking? Even I have lines. Having a shipment change hands in my city when I have advance notice of it is unacceptable. You're taking out the buyer and the seller tonight. I want to send a message to anyone who even thinks about running people through my city."

I appreciate his sentiments but . . . he's got one thing wrong.

"I don't take orders from you," I reply. "That's not how we work anymore."

He narrows his nearly black gaze on me. "Then consider this returning the favor that I did for you."

Ransom said he was closing in on Lagarto, so there's a fucking good chance I already need to be there. As soon as I get out of this cell-phone dead spot that's Mount's office, I'll get in touch with him to find out where the hell he's at.

"I take the job, and then we're even."

"Fine. As long as you end this. Tonight."

"It'll be done."

FORTY-FOUR
TEMPERANCE

K ane isn't returning my texts or calls, and I'm starting to worry. Skip starting, my mind is already running down all the rabbit holes of what could have possibly happened to him.

He's fine. He's capable. He's probably just doing recon or something and turned his phone off.

I rationalize his silence any way I can as I pace my apartment, staring down at the app Ariel installed on my phone that allows me to track Magnolia. I don't know how Ariel did it, but as long as Magnolia has her phone on her, I know where she is.

She's been to the club and is now at her downtown penthouse. I can't confirm any of my crazy suspicions until I talk to her, but I don't want to confront her without Kane. I have no doubt that she's dangerous.

And my fucking brother . . . he might be on a

mission to kill his goddamned girlfriend and doesn't even know it.

I don't know how she could have pulled it off, but she's wily as hell.

There's only one other person I can call who might be able to shed some light on the situation, but I hesitate. It's Sunday night, and my questions will certainly be unwelcome.

But what other choice do I have?

I exit the app and tap on my former boss's contact. Keira knows Magnolia better than anyone.

"Hey, Temperance. Is something wrong?"

I suppose that would be my first reaction if she were calling me on a Sunday night too, so it's fair.

"That's what I'm trying to figure out. Can I ask you about someone?"

She goes quiet for a beat. "You know I can't and won't tell you anything about Mount."

"No, no, of course not. And that's not what I'm after."

"Then who?"

"Magnolia."

The line goes silent for a long moment. "Maybe. What do you want to know?"

When I hang up with Keira, instead of feeling relieved, I find my apprehension has hit a new level. The final nail in my coffin of hope that my suspicions might be wrong? Keira's last statement.

"Magnolia has been through things you can't imagine. Don't underestimate her."

Something is seriously wrong here, and all roads lead back to Magnolia.

I reopen the app that I had tracking her, and the red marker has moved.

Where the hell are you going, Magnolia?

She's heading out of town but sticking along the river.

I'm not full of conspiracy theories like Ariel, but it doesn't take a mind like hers to come up with a few ideas about what could possibly be happening down by the Mississippi on a Sunday night.

Human trafficking.

My stomach clenches into a tight knot, and I try Kane again with no answer.

"Where are you?" I ask the empty room. "What the hell am I supposed to do? Let this happen and do nothing?"

Obviously, the room doesn't answer me, but I already know one thing.

I can't let this happen.

I pull on black leggings, a black T-shirt, and boots, and make sure the gun in my purse is loaded. I don't know what I'm walking into, but I'm going to be prepared.

My phone rings as I slide into the front seat of the Audi. *Kane.*

"Thank God you're okay. I've been trying to get you for hours."

"Meeting ran long. Only have a minute. Lay low tonight. I'll get home when I can."

"But—"

"I'll explain everything when I get home. I swear I'm not keeping anything from you, but I have to handle this myself. I'm going dark for a few hours. I promise I'll be safe. I love you, Temperance."

The call ends, and Kane is gone. I try to call him right back but the phone goes straight to voice mail.

He must have called me and then immediately turned his phone off. I'm smart enough to read between the lines. He's not going to be reachable or traceable. He has a job. A hit.

Fuck. What if he's going after Lagarto . . . and he doesn't know it's Magnolia?

I flip to the app again and check Magnolia's position. She's still sticking along the road that winds along the river. If Kane can't stop whatever she's doing, I will.

FORTY-FIVE

KANE

This is the last time.
My last job.

I know it when I walk out of Mount's office and immediately call Temperance.

Before, I had nothing to lose. Now, I have everything.

There's no question in my mind that if I wanted to keep living this life, Temperance could handle it. But I don't want her to. I carry no guilt for the things I've done, but I don't need to keep doing them. I have more money than we'll be able to spend in a lifetime. Our children, if we have them, will be set for life too.

A vision of Temperance pregnant with a little girl who'll look just like her forms in my mind as I drive toward an old warehouse by the river that's bank owned and the perfect place to transfer a load of human cargo. The closer I get, the more real the vision becomes—so real that I have to block it out because it's too pure for where I'm going and what I'm going to do.

Before I pull off the side of the road about a quarter mile beyond the warehouse and park behind an abandoned building, another picture blooms in my brain— my mom holding her granddaughter.

I wish I could give her that.

I pop the trunk and exit the car silently before collecting my sniper rifle from the hidden compartment.

This isn't my first rodeo, but it's going to be my last.

I keep to the shadows as I move quietly in the direction of the location Mount gave me, but the hair on the back of my neck stands up.

Something doesn't feel right.

Stopping, I listen for movement, hoping like hell I'm not about to get ambushed or that this isn't a double cross.

Mount hasn't fucked me over yet, but if he's determined for some reason that I'm at the end of my useful life, he wouldn't hesitate to take me out.

But I can't see him sending me into the dark to make it happen. He'd put a bullet between my eyes like a real man.

The sound of a truck rumbles up ahead, the old diesel motor vibrating the rusted mailbox near the gate entrance. I duck into the bushes as headlights cut through the falling dusk.

You'd think human trafficking would take place at night, in the pitch black, and some of it does. But plenty of it happens during broad daylight, in plain sight. This handoff, if that's really what I'm walking into, is something in between. Early evening but still out of the way, where they think no one will see them. But I will, once I figure out where the fuck this is going down and what the right spot is.

This is one more reason I don't take short-notice contracts. I never want to be surprised when I set up to do a job. I want to know the location of every entrance, exit, traffic pattern, security guard, security camera, fence line, and crack in the pavement.

There's a reason I'm the best at what I do, and why I command a high price.

And now I'm walking up on human traffickers with no recon.

Fucking stupid.

Part of me wants to turn around and tell Mount to fuck off, but when I see the small bus turn into the open gate with a yellow WEST PARK CARE CENTER on the side, I know I can't.

I'd do this job for free.

FORTY-SIX
TEMPERANCE

I guide the Audi down the same road Magnolia traveled, and with each passing mile, I wonder what the hell I'm doing. I've done dumber things, but not for a very long time. Although, maybe this takes the cake. My nausea has passed and so have any other pregnancy symptoms. So . . . it was probably a false alarm.

I put that out of my mind because there's nothing I can do either way. Instead, I focus on the situation at hand, which is the smartest choice.

I've been trying to piece all of this together, but it's like trying to work on a puzzle without a box. Frustrating and time consuming.

The dot on the app keeps moving, but instead of going further, now it's driving around in what seems to be circles.

"Please, God, tell me she's not freaking lost."

I know I can't possibly get lucky enough that

Magnolia is changing her mind about where she's going, maybe due to a guilty conscience, but I can still hope.

Or she already picked up the people and is moving them.

My skin crawls at the thought of Magnolia trafficking people.

But she sells women . . . so despite her protests and explanation, is it really that unthinkable that she wouldn't take this next step?

Unless I'm wrong and she's just looking for a trendy restaurant that's hip and hot and located outside of town? Yeah, I'm not that dumb either.

My gut says something bad is happening here, and if I'm wrong, then I can go home and wait for Kane and pretend I didn't go off on some crazy goose chase.

And then the dot makes one last turn toward the river and stops.

Where the hell are you, Magnolia? And is Kane out here too?

FORTY-SEVEN
KANE

From my perch on a rusty shipping container in the back corner of the shipyard, I've got my sight on the bus from the old folks' home as it sits idling, and a black Suburban pulls up behind it and parks.

A boat motor drones in the distance, and through my scope, I get a closer look. It looks like a dozen people in orange life jackets, and SANDY'S SWAMP TOURS is painted along the side of the boat in big yellow letters.

Mount wants me to take out the buyer and the seller. How I'm going to know who is who, I have no fucking idea.

Another reason I don't take a contract without research.

Someone important is in the SUV. If it's Giles, I'll finally get the chance I've been waiting for to take him out.

The boat pulls up next to the seawall, and a man climbs out of the bus to help them dock.

Before anyone can get off the boat, a BMW SUV hauls ass through the gate and slams on its brakes just before it T-bones the black Suburban, and the doors of both vehicles fly open.

A woman jumps out of the BMW and starts waving her hands and yelling.

What in the actual fuck?

I blink twice, and it takes me a full second to recognize her in the fading sunlight.

Magnolia Maison.

Jesus fucking Christ.

Mount sent me to eliminate the madam.

FORTY-EIGHT
TEMPERANCE

I floor the Audi and blow past the little red dot that signifies Magnolia's location.

Shit.

I turn into another driveway and back out, moving slowly as I approach again.

It's a warehouse that looks like it's about to fall down any second. Shipping containers are piled high in a parking lot, some with the doors wide open.

If I were a human trafficker, this is probably where I would be.

I pass it again before I pull off to the side of the road and cut the engine.

This is quite clearly the dumbest thing I've ever done in my life. I'm not getting out of this car.

I'm just not.

Kane would kill me.

I pick up my phone and try him again for what feels like the twentieth time, but it goes straight to voice mail.

Dammit, Kane, where are you? Are you here?

I don't need him to always come charging to my rescue, but when faced with a situation that's a thousand levels out of my league, it would be nice to be able to get in touch with the man who handles stuff like this all the time.

I stare down at my phone and have one other last-ditch idea. But before I can tap my brother's contact, the yelling starts.

I open the door to hear more clearly.

Magnolia. She's hollering up a storm.

"Let go of me, Giles! Don't you fucking touch me! I'm gonna kill you both if you set me up!"

Kill you both?

As in . . . Giles and . . .

Shit. Rafe is supposed to be ending this. Which means . . .

Jesus fucking Christ.

I'm not going to let Magnolia kill my brother. I glance at the shipping containers. *But if Kane is here . . . he won't let her.*

Kane will never pull the trigger on a woman. I know that.

Fuck.

I slide my gun from its holster in my purse, get out of the Audi, and head toward what I hope isn't my first kill. I only make it two steps before I freeze as Magnolia screams again.

"Rafe! Where the fuck are you? You lying bastard! I'm going to kill you myself!"

No.

No.

No.

FORTY-NINE
KANE

J*esus fucking Christ.* I don't know what the hell is happening right here, right now, but I know it's not what I expected to see.

Giles jumps out of the Suburban and grabs Magnolia Maison, who is thrashing around too much for me to take my shot at him.

Fucking woman.

She better not be the other target. Mount has to know I won't kill her. That's dirty work he'll have to do himself.

When she starts screaming Ransom's name, my finger freezes where it hovers over the trigger.

What. The. Fuck.

Temperance's brother hops off the boat, leaving another man on board with the ten women in life jackets, and walks toward Magnolia.

Please tell me I'm fucking wrong about what's happening here.
Please tell me Ransom is about to double-cross them and—

He pulls a gun from his back pocket, but he doesn't point it at Giles, he points it directly at Magnolia.

"What the fuck are you doing here, Mags?"

"I came because you fucking set me up to take the fall for this." She attempts to wave a hand. "All this time . . . you were the motherfucking Lizard."

No fucking way. That motherfucker did not play me.

No. I refuse to fucking believe it.

Ransom has been hunting the Lizard. He can't be the Lizard.

I watch through the scope, and I know I'm wrong the minute he smiles and spits a wad of dip in the dirt. "I thought it meant alligator, actually. But languages aren't my thing."

Fucking Shit.

I keep the crosshairs on Ransom's head and my finger rests on the trigger, but I can't do it.

Temperance will never forgive me if I do it. She will never understand. I'll never be able to explain this to her.

Especially because I don't know how I missed it myself. *Ransom fucking played us all.* Even his own goddamned sister.

"How could you lie to me?" Magnolia's voice carries through the quiet night.

"Why the hell are you here?" Ransom asks.

"Mount." Magnolia bites out his name. "Apparently he wanted me to see for myself what a piece of shit you really are." She waves an arm at the women in the boat. "How could you?"

That motherfucker. Is that why he sent me? Because he wanted me to protect Magnolia while she confronted Ransom?

There are too many unanswered questions and complications for me to do a fucking thing.

Which Mount had to know.

Why didn't he tell me Ransom was the target?

It takes me all of half a second to answer that question.

He knew I'd never do it if he told me.

But now, faced with the prospect of letting the man I thought I knew kill a woman who is screaming at him about lying to her . . . the choice becomes muddy.

I only have one option, and it's the one thing a sniper should never, ever fucking do.

Abandon my position and move in to take care of this face-to-face.

I pop the round out of the rifle and eject the magazine before leaving the rifle on top of the container and checking my sidearm.

None of this is happening at a distance.

I climb down from the shipping container to make my way toward the clusterfuck unfolding between the occupants of the BMW and the Suburban.

"Mount never could mind his own business," Ransom says, staring at Magnolia. "It wasn't supposed to happen like this. You were never supposed to know. It was one last job, and I was done. We were going to have a life."

"Is that why Mount's guy found accounts in my name in the Cayman Islands? Accounts taking payments for the shit you've been pinning on me? Why the fuck would you do that if you weren't setting me up?" Magnolia's tone is desperate, bordering on hysterically pissed.

"Baby, you gotta believe me. Everything I did was for you. For us."

"Don't you dare tell me you're selling *women* to help *me*. You know what I've been through. You know I have lines. You know I would never fucking sink so low."

Ransom's tone changes completely. "Come on, Mags. We both know you're barely a half step above this. You peddle pussy. What makes you think some of your girls didn't come from me?"

Her head rears back, and she roars.

"I'm going to fucking kill you, Rafe Ransom!"

FIFTY
TEMPERANCE

I suck in a sharp breath, but it feels like the air is laced with razor blades.

No.

No.

No.

I'm not hearing what I'm hearing.

This isn't happening.

It's a nightmare.

"You're gonna judge me? You, of all people." My brother's booming laugh rings out, sounding harsh and fake. "You're a fucking joke, Mags. You're a whore who sells whores. You're no better than me. That's why we fit together so well."

Magnolia yanks her arm away from Giles and swings her fist, and it glances off my brother's jaw. Giles reaches out and grabs her by the throat.

"No!"

Everyone freezes at the screamed word, including me.

"Who the fuck was that?" Rafe looks around, and so does Giles as I cringe.

Oh sweet Jesus. What the hell is wrong with me?

Giles releases Magnolia, shoving her at Rafe. I duck behind the container and run—directly into a hard chest.

Another scream breaks free from my throat before a large hand clamps over my mouth. I look up into piercing blue eyes.

Kane.

He pulls me in close to his chest before spinning us around to move—but it's too late.

From behind me, Giles speaks. "I got 'em, Ransom. Both of them."

FIFTY-ONE
KANE

My worst fucking nightmare is playing out in front of me.

The prospect of killing Temperance's brother seems like a walk in the park compared to holding her against my side as we're led at gunpoint by Giles toward the SUVs.

I could have pulled the gun tucked into the back of my jeans and ended him where he stands, but not with Temperance in the line of fire. No fucking way.

Ransom won't let him kill her. Me, sure. But not his sister. I'm one hundred percent sure of that. *Jesus fuck.* I never thought Ransom was smart enough to pull off this kind of con.

Never underestimate a smuggler.

"What the fuck? Tempe?" Ransom shoves Magnolia to the ground as we stop in front of him.

"Rafe? What are you doing? Please tell me this isn't what it looks like. Please."

Temperance's begging slices at my heart, and I hate this for her. I hate it even worse than I hated pulling the trigger in the airport in front of her.

"Tempe, what the hell are you doing here?" Ransom's face is creased with confusion, at least until he meets my gaze. "I know there's no fucking way Saxon would bring you here with him." He shakes his head. "What the fuck, man? Thought you'd do a better job of protecting her."

"Let your sister leave. Right the fuck now." There's no mistaking my statements for anything but what they are—nonnegotiable.

Ransom tilts his head, a new light entering his eyes. "Now why would I do that? As long as she's here, I've got you by the balls. I never figured when I hooked you two up, she'd fall so fucking hard for you. But you, Saxon. I knew you'd never be able to resist her. Loner with no one who has ever given a shit about you. And then Temperance comes along, and you take the bait like a catfish to chicken liver."

"What?" Temperance whispers. "*You* set us up? You sent the note?"

Ransom nods and jerks his chin at Magnolia, where she's staring up at him from the ground like he's sprouted horns and cloven hooves. She might not be far off.

"Stole Mags's stationery from the club. Wasn't no

hard thing. I wondered if I wrote too sloppy and you'd recognize it as mine. But you didn't even question it. Just trotted right off and fell into line."

This motherfucker.

"You sent me to a sex club? Because you wanted to set me up with a hit man? What the hell, Rafe? And then you come warn me about going back?"

I can hear the tears she's fighting off, and now I wish I'd taken the shot when I had the chance. No one, not even Rafe Ransom, makes Temperance cry.

"You think I don't know you? If I warned you off, you'd be twice as likely to go back. Stubborn as fuck, that's what you've always been."

"Why? Why all of these crazy schemes?"

"Money," Giles says from behind us. "He could never get enough. Always needed more to make sure he'd never be that broke kid in the swamp again."

"We didn't need more money, asshole!" Magnolia scoots back in the gravel, and Giles lunges for her.

Ransom pulls his gun and I reach for mine, thinking he's going to pull the trigger on Magnolia, but he puts a bullet in Giles's head instead.

What. The. Fuck?

"Never liked that pretentious douchebag," Ransom says absently, staring down at Giles's body.

When Ransom looks back up at Temperance and me, he's looking down the barrel of my gun.

FIFTY-TWO
TEMPERANCE

"Now I keep the money and the girls. Sell them to a higher bidder," Ransom says with a smile.

"That's what you did with your last shipment. Isn't it, Ransom?" Kane's question clicks into my brain, and all of a sudden it makes sense.

"Oh my God. Tell me he's wrong. Tell me that's not what happened."

"Tell your boyfriend to drop the fucking gun unless you want me to unload the rest of these rounds into his chest in front of you."

"Temperance, back away," Kane orders.

My brother apparently still knows one aspect of my personality better than Kane, because instead of stepping aside, I lunge in front of Kane, blocking any potential shot Rafe could take.

"Temperance, you better—"

"You made me watch you *die*, and it was all because

you wanted to make more money?" My voice grows shrill and cracks. "How many lives have you ruined, Rafe? How could you do this? My brother couldn't do this!"

"Tempe—"

I shake my head. I'm staring at a stranger.

"All for money? Really?" I whisper. "Put the gun down. Let them go. Let us all leave. And then just fucking disappear, because I don't need a brother anymore. Not if he could do something like that."

Rafe's eyes turn hard. "You think you're so much better than me? You grew up in that swamp the same fucking way I did. We're the same."

"We are not the same!"

"No, maybe not. Because I'm not standing in front of a killer trying to pretend he's better than your brother. Saxon's only here because Mount gave an order to his favorite executioner. You can live with loving a hit man, but you want to pretend I don't exist for what I've done? I don't think so."

He raises his gun higher, over my head, and Kane shoves me aside.

I hit the gravel as the shots explode in the night.

FIFTY-THREE
TEMPERANCE

"I'm so sorry, Temperance." Magnolia's hand shakes as she lowers her small pink pistol.

Magnolia shot my brother. She shot my brother. And Kane—

"Kane!" I scream as I bolt to where he's lying on the ground. "Please, God. I can't do this again. You can't be dead. I won't allow it."

I refuse to look at my brother yet as I check Kane for injuries. His palm traps mine against his chest.

"I'm not gonna die. Not this time."

"Oh my God. You scared the hell out of me."

He glances down at his shoulder. "Flesh wound."

I find the blood weeping from the small tear in his shirt, and breathe a sigh of relief. It's not mortal.

Kane looks beyond me, and I don't want to turn around. I can't turn around.

Magnolia is over there, and so are two dead bodies.

"I'm so sorry."

She whispers it over and over, and my heart is breaking. This time, it's infinitely worse than the airport, because I feel every single rip as my soul shreds into pieces. I turn to face my brother, but he's not dead.

He lifts his hand, reaching out toward me. "Tempe. Please."

He's not dead.

I scramble toward him and drop to my knees as blood pools in the gravel.

"I'm sorry," he says. "I didn't . . . I didn't . . . want you to see this. It wasn't supposed to be like this."

Blood trickles from the corner of his mouth, and I hold up my fingers as Kane kneels beside me and uses his shirt to put pressure on his chest wounds—his very real chest wounds this time.

"Don't talk." I look at Magnolia. "Call nine one one. Now!"

She reaches for her phone as I look back down at Rafe.

"Help is coming. You're going to be fine."

My brother might have betrayed us all, but he's still my flesh and blood. He might have made horrible choices that I will never understand, but no one and nothing is going to prevent me from trying to save him.

He's the only family I have.

"I ain't got much time. Got things to say."

Tears drip down my cheeks. Magnolia's voice blurs into the background noise of the night as I focus completely on my brother. "No. You're not dying, dammit."

He pulls my hand close to his face. "So fucking sorry. I just wanted to be somebody."

"You didn't have to be anyone but yourself! You didn't have to do this!"

He nods. "It was always gonna end like this. I just wish you weren't here to see it. Wish I didn't have to put you through this twice." He coughs, and the rattle in his chest turns my blood cold.

"Rafe, please."

"It's better this way. You found yourself a new life. Be happy, Tempe. Live."

He coughs again, and his gaze loses focus.

"Take good care of her or I'll haunt you . . ." His words trail off as his eyes roll back.

"No!" I scream.

Kane clutches me tight against him, like he's trying to keep me from breaking into pieces. But it's too late.

I'm already shattered.

FIFTY-FOUR
TEMPERANCE

Magnolia didn't call 911. She called Mount.

And when the cavalry shows up, Mount orders one of his men to take the women somewhere in the bus, and then tells Kane to take me home and for one of his guys to drive the Audi back to the warehouse, where a doctor will meet us to see to Kane's wound.

Ten minutes after the doctor leaves, I sink to the floor in Kane's shower, watching red water circle the drain as the last of my tears trickle down my cheeks. My chest aches from my heart breaking.

My brother betrayed us all. The brother who protected me. Stood up for me. Helped me.

I can't reconcile his actions with who I've always known him to be.

What's more, I don't want to.

Hot water washes over me, and I wish it could wash

my memories clean. Keep them from being tainted by the events of tonight.

But nothing can do that.

The last time I grieved my brother, my guilt compounded everything. I thought I'd led him to his death by letting Kane use me to get to him, but nothing could have been further from the truth. This time, I won't get so lucky.

These facts are facts, and there's nothing I can do to change them.

The bathroom door opens.

"You need anything?" Kane asks as he sticks his head inside.

As soon as he sees me on the floor, pain lances through his expression as he comes toward the enclosure, not even bothering to strip off his clothes before he reaches the door. Once he's inside, he crouches and wraps his arms around me.

"I'm so fucking sorry." Kane lifts me into his lap, unhampered by his superglued wound, and rocks me, holding me tight as the water soaks us both.

"I'm sorry."

"Why?"

I press my face against his neck. "Because you wouldn't have been part of this mess if my brother hadn't dragged you in."

"Shh. That's not on you. None of it's on you. Besides . . ."

"What?"

"We really should be thanking your brother, because without him, we wouldn't be here."

I hadn't thought about it like that, but in a way, Kane's right.

Rafe orchestrated all of this. Like some criminal mastermind.

I push that part out of my head and focus on the man whose arms are wrapped around me.

The last time I thought my brother died, I thought I was all alone in the world, but this time, he left me a gift.

"Hold me a little longer?"

"As long as you want, princess. I'm not going anywhere."

Early the next morning, as Kane keeps me pressed against his side, I roll over and my stomach stages a revolt.

Shit.

I jump out of bed and bolt for the bathroom, barely making it in time.

Kane is on my heels. "Are you okay? What's wrong?"

I glance over my shoulder to find he's got a gun in his hand. I wave at him and heave again. Seconds later, there's a cold cloth on my forehead.

When my stomach finally calms down, I reach for the washcloth and use it to wipe my mouth. Kane helps me off my knees, and I turn to face his lined expression, trying to find the words that I wasn't ready to say.

"I think . . . There's a chance . . . I could maybe . . . It's possible that . . ."

"You're pregnant?"

FIFTY-FIVE
KANE

My vision of Temperance from yesterday, when the thought of her pregnant flashed through my mind, comes back full force, nearly knocking me off my feet.

"You're pregnant?" I ask again, just in case she didn't hear my question the first time.

From the look on her face, she didn't miss it. "I don't know. I haven't . . . I was going to take a test."

"And you didn't even mention the possibility to me?"

"I didn't want to freak you out if it wasn't true."

I step closer and pull her against my body. "What part of this do you think freaks me out?"

"The part where we've never talked about kids. If you want them. If they could possibly fit into your life."

I tilt her chin up so I can look her in her brown eyes. "If you want kids, I want them with you. As for them fitting in my life, I'm done with all of it. I told Mount this was my last job. The only part that freaks me out is the part where you *walked your ass into a gunfight thinking you could be pregnant.*" I keep my tone as calm as possible.

"I wasn't sure. I just . . . I wasn't going to go. But then I heard Magnolia yelling . . ."

I already know what Temperance is going to say. "You heard your brother's name."

She nods, her eyes filling with tears again. "I still don't understand how he could've . . ."

"Shh . . . Don't. That could be why you're making yourself sick."

She bites down on her lip and pulls herself together. "We need to make a run to the pharmacy."

FIFTY-SIX
TEMPERANCE

I never knew two minutes could be so damn long. *Never.*

"Thirty seconds," Kane says, squeezing my hand.

His words definitely calmed some of my concerns about the possibility of me being pregnant, especially the part where he said he was done with this part of his life.

I meet that icy blue gaze I've come to adore more than life itself. "No matter what, it's you and me against the world. Deal?"

Kane's lips stretch in a smile. "No matter what. I love you, Temperance."

"Not more than I love you."

He pulls me against his side, and together we walk toward the counter where the test lays.

Holy shit.

It's positive.

EPILOGUE
KANE

Eighteen months later

When we drive through town, the first thing I notice is that the Giles name has been removed from all the buildings it used to grace. I suppose Mount arranging for Giles's body to be found with a boatload of evidence of his involvement with human trafficking will motivate a city to forget the family name.

Still hard to believe we're here.

"You sure this is where you want to live? We could go anywhere."

My wife—my beautiful, incredible wife—looks over at me from the passenger seat of the SUV.

"I already bought the house. There's no changing my mind now." Temperance glances up in the rearview mirror to look in the backseat at our sleeping twin girls. "They're going to love it here."

At the stop sign, I look over my shoulder. Just like every time I see them, I can't help but smile. *We did that.*

Fucking miracles.

I also married their mama before they were born, and because we were on an island in the middle of the South Pacific, I was able to give her my name.

When we came back, we learned that Temperance's girl Ariel had wiped much of the history of my death off the internet, but it still doesn't wipe people's minds clean. I'm Ken Sax, an avid day trader to the rest of the world, because it will never be safe for me to live as Kane Savage. It doesn't bother me, though, because I have a life I could never have dreamed of the day I adopted my alias.

I don't know how I let Temperance talk me into moving into a house out on acreage just one town over from where I grew up. *Oh, wait. Yes, I do. She was naked.* All joking aside, there's nothing I wouldn't give any of my girls.

"Turn up here. It's down about a mile, on the right."

I've yet to see the house she picked, but it doesn't matter what it looks like as long as I have my family with me.

It's been eighteen months since my official retirement, which means I've had time to watch Temperance shine as her career took off like a rocket headed for the moon. She's been working through her brother's betrayal one piece at a time, and the emotion fuels her. There's a piece of that grief in every single sculpture she makes, but a little less each time.

The waiting list for a Temperance Ransom original is over a year long. Together, we've created a totally new life for ourselves and the girls—and it feels good. Damn good.

Temperance points out the mailbox, and I turn down the long paved driveway until I see a big yellow house at the end that looks like someone dipped it in sunshine.

I glance at my wife, and she smiles.

Fitting.

She's brought me into the light. No more shadows.

I lean over and steal a kiss. "I love it."

Her grin widens. "I knew you would. Ready to see the inside?"

"Let's split up the troops and check it out."

Temperance
Six months later

"Thank you so much, Nan. I appreciate it more than you know."

Our next-door neighbor, Nan Prather, gives me a hug. "Like I would ever turn down the chance to babysit those little girls. I swear, they've given me a second lease on life. I always wanted grandbabies of my own."

It guts me that I can't tell Kane's mom that I picked this house so she could have her family back.

Her son.

Her grandbabies.

The daughter-in-law she probably never thought she'd get to hug.

But how do you explain to someone why her son had to fake his death over a decade and a half ago and could never tell her he was alive?

When Kane realized who our next-door neighbors were—his mom and the man his dad asked to watch over them both—I thought he might shake me. But he didn't.

He got really quiet, swept a hand over Adrianna's downy-soft hair and stared at Lauren. Finally, after about five minutes, he told me, "You did right, princess. She loves these girls. I would've given this to her if I could've found a way how. You knew that, and you found the way."

He stepped away from our daughters and wrapped his hand around my neck, bringing his lips to my forehead.

"You always give me exactly what I need."

When I look into Nan's blue eyes, I see so much of Kane there. She and Jeremiah are thrilled to be the twins' honorary grandparents, but I would give anything for Nan to know there's nothing honorary about it.

Maybe someday.

Kane

"Thank you so much, ma'am." I take the diaper bag Temperance left inside from Ma's hands. *Nan's hands.* I always have to correct myself, but it never seems to stick. "We really appreciate you watching the girls. Means the world to us."

"Means the world to me too."

She smiles, and seeing the joy on her face that has been there every time she's watched my babies has healed my soul in a way nothing else could.

I feel so fucking blessed to have this life that I shouldn't have been allowed.

It's all because of Temperance.

"Thank you again," I say as I turn for the door.

"It's really not a problem, Kane."

I freeze in midstep.

"You think I wouldn't know my own boy? I've been waiting six months for you to tell me, and I think I've waited long enough."

Slowly, I turn around, and that joy is still on her face. Along with knowledge.

"You think a mother wouldn't know? I don't care if it was fifteen years or fifty, I would always know my boy."

A lump rises in my throat. "How long have you known?"

"Since the first time you cursed and checked yourself in front of me. Same way you always did when you were minding your manners. Then there's your girls—they have the same eyes you did when you were their age. A mother just knows."

"I'm so sorry, Ma. So fucking sorry." I rush toward her and gather her into a hug.

"Don't you apologize for anything. Not now. Not ever. You gave me everything when you changed the course of my life. Another man I love and who loves me with every breath in his body. And now, two grandbabies and a daughter to spoil. I have *everything* because you gave up the world for me."

I bow my head as tears drip down my cheeks onto her face, mingling with hers. "I love you, Ma."

"I know, Kane. I've always known."

When I walk out of the house and Temperance sees my face, she rushes toward me.

"What's wrong?"

I wrap my arms around her and squeeze hard. "Nothing."

"She knows, doesn't she?"

I nod silently, because that lump in my throat won't budge.

When I release my hold on my wife, I drop to my knees, and my baby girls crawl toward me.

I bow my head and give thanks to whoever was handing out second chances to broken men the day I got mine.

I may not deserve this life, but I will never take it for granted.

I am whole again.

The End

ACKNOWLEDGMENTS

Wow. This was a doozy. I feel like I say that every time, and it seems to be the case lately. One would think it would get easier after twenty-something books, but it doesn't. As always, this book did not magically flow from my fingertips into the form it is in now. It took a small army to help me take this story from my brain to the pages you're reading. Massive thanks go out to my team:

Jacob Wilson—You're not just on the cover, your influence is visible on so many of these pages. You are my love, my best friend, and my rock. Thank you for embracing our journey and teaching me every day what romance truly is. I love you.

Pam Berehulke—Thank you for your patience, eye for detail, and professionalism. You are an integral part of my team, and I can't imagine doing this without you! (Also, please never stop editing books, because I don't know what I would do without you.)

Jamie Lynn—Thank you for handling all the details when I'm living in my head and dreaming about fictional characters. I love having you on #Team-Awesome.

Kim and Natasha—Thank you for believing in this story, even when I was struggling, and giving me your honest insight. You helped me make these babies shine!

Julie Deaton—Your eagle eyes are incredible! Thank you for your fabulous proofreading.

My readers—Thank you for trusting me and taking a chance on a story when I can tell you almost nothing about it going in. I hope you enjoyed it as much as I loved bringing Temperance and Kane's story to life. I can't wait to tell you about what's coming next!

Amazing bloggers—Thank you for everything you do so tirelessly and with such passion. I see you. I appreciate you. I am so grateful. Thank you a million times over.

ALSO BY MEGHAN MARCH

MAGNOLIA DUET:

Creole Kingpin

Madam Temptress

LEGEND TRILOGY:

The Fall of Legend

House of Scarlett

The Fight for Forever

DIRTY MAFIA DUET:

Black Sheep

White Knight

FORGE TRILOGY:

Deal with the Devil

Luck of the Devil

Heart of the Devil

SIN TRILOGY:

Richer Than Sin

Guilty as Sin

Reveling in Sin

MOUNT TRILOGY:

Ruthless King

Defiant Queen

Sinful Empire

SAVAGE TRILOGY:

Savage Prince

Iron Princess

Rogue Royalty

BENEATH SERIES:

Beneath This Mask

Beneath This Ink

Beneath These Chains

Beneath These Scars

Beneath These Lies

Beneath These Shadows

Beneath The Truth

DIRTY BILLIONAIRE TRILOGY:

Dirty Billionaire

Dirty Pleasures

Dirty Together

DIRTY GIRL DUET:

Dirty Girl

Dirty Love

ABOUT THE AUTHOR

Making the jump from corporate lawyer to romance author was a leap of faith that *New York Times*, #1 *Wall Street Journal*, and *USA Today* bestselling author Meghan March will never regret. With over thirty titles published, she has sold millions of books in nearly a dozen languages to fellow romance-lovers around the world. A nomad at heart, she can currently be found in the woods of the Pacific Northwest, living her happily ever after with her real-life alpha hero.

She would love to hear from you.
Connect with her at:
www.meghanmarch.com

Printed in Great Britain
by Amazon

83958122R00161